The Available Wife

A NOVEL BY Carla PENNINGTON

The Available Wife

Carla
PENNINGTON

Life Changing Books in conjunction with Power Play Media
Published by Life Changing Books
P.O. Box 423 Brandywine, MD 20613

Library of Congress Cataloging-in-Publication Data;

www.lifechangingbooks.net
13 Digit: 978-1934230176
10 Digit: 1-934230170

Acknowledgements

First and foremost, I give praises to the Almighty. Without him blessing me with this gift, none of this would be possible. You have pulled me through some tumultuous times and never given up on me even when I started giving up on myself. Thank you, God!

To my grandparents, Ollie and Rosie Brown (may they rest in peace), thank you for rescuing me. I love you and I miss you dearly. *Tears*

To my number one fan, my mama, Rosa Pennington Browne, I love you. I think I can put that little girl to rest now that you've reentered my life. Thank you for coming back to me.

To my dad, Carl Pennington, we've been down some rough roads but we're back. I love you!

To my crumbsnatchers, Kemyria, Kemberlyn, Jevon (Ju-Boy), I love you with all my heart. Thank you for all the laughs and fun that you have brought into my life. My life would be empty if you three weren't a part of it. Mommy is doing this for you. Soon, we will be boarding that Nickelodeon cruise ship!

My family…WHEW! Aunt Lela Brown Braggs, I will need a whole page to tell you how much I appreciate you and everything that you have done for me and continue to do. When I needed a mother, you were there. Though brutal at times, you taught me the ropes and what to watch for in the world. You never sugarcoated anything with me. You kept it real and I appreciate that dearly. Although I'm grown with three kids, I still look to you for guidance and I never want to disappoint you and I hope I never will. I love you!

Aunt Arvetta "Arby" Washington, thank you for everything that you have done for me and mine. We may have butted heads at times, but you will always be my Arby. I will always remember and cherish those times as a little girl when I would come to your house and you'd have a big pot of crabs just for me. Here I am, a grown woman, and you still spoil me in such a way. I love you and don't ever change. You have a heart of gold!

Aunt Linda Sue Brown and Aunt Mary Jackson, thank you for loving me, being there for me, believing in me and steering me straight. I love you dearly.

To my uncles, Abraham Brown, Ollie Brown Jr., Jimmie Brown and Boo Boo, thank you for being more than just my uncles. You love me sternly but mean no harm. I love you!

My big sister, Kimberly Pennington Saxton, we may fight and fuss but in the end, it's all love! You've been a huge supporter in my life as well as my writing journey. From day one, you were there and you helped me see it through 'til the end. You were a thorn in my side but you pushed until I got it done. Guess what? It's done! I love you!

My brother, Bryan, thank you for coming back. My brousin, Aaron Brown, thank you for being my cousin and brother!

My girls who have rolled with me through thick and thin, heat and cold, tears and laughter, etc. Rashunda White, we have been through some thangs but it's always been me and you, baby! Enough said!

Krystal Jiles, my "den mother," my right when I wanna be wrong, thank you for being you and thank you for keeping me out of trouble when I wanted to get into some.

LaTonya McCants, I'm ready to hit Vegas when you are! We've rolled and kicked it like no others. Wouldn't trade any of it for the world.

Kimberly Thompson, thank you for listening and giving it to me straight!

Kimberly Burden, it's on, trique! Thank you for all the good times we've shared and continue to share! We got thangs to do, baby girl!

Anna Phillips, we strayed but we found each other again and I am happy that we did. I love you, cousin!
Simetra Brown, my quiet friend, thank you for being a part of my life.

Valencia Wortham (Meagan Rebecca), thank you for being my play-play proof reader and play-play assistant but heifer, I need you to tell me what's wrong with the stories. LOL!

Tennille Thomas, thank you for being my girl. Ride or die!

Shanavie R. Thomas, thank you for having a hand in getting me fired for printing out my stories at work. It was worth it, chic. LOL!

To my boys, Gemini Bailey (Curtis), thank you for always having my back. We will always be "us" no matter what. Wesley "Chuckie" Young, thank you for always being there to talk to me and curse me out when I needed it.

Tommie Holmes, we need to hurry back to Florida for more lottery tickets. Thank you for all your help.

Herbert Miller, we're still misunderstood but who gives a damn. You're my boy! Always! Dennis Akins (D-Ray), thank you for keeping it real with me and being there for me.

Shawn Pipkins, we met at a crazy time in my life, but we clicked. I can't wait 'til the day that I actually "meet" you. You better not disappear on me again.

Craig Warden, I'll be in ATL soon. Look out for me!

Commie Hobbs, thank you for the talks and definitely the laughs.

Leon Smith, which Ne-Yo song do you want me to pick? We've been through them all! Words can't express how much you mean to me and how much you have helped me. I will keep it simple because that's what you like so, Thank you!

Carmen Coleman, thank you for all that you've done. You're greatly appreciated.

Stephanie Tullos Tsikrikas, I haven't forgotten about you. I will keep my promise.

To my LCB crew, I'm so happy to be a part of this family and I owe it all to Juicy Wright. Thank you for paying it forward. Not many people would have done what you did, but you did. A simple act of kindness goes a long way. Thank you so much.

Boss lady Tressa, thank you for giving me the opportunity to be a part of this family. It really means a lot and I will not disappoint.

Leslie Allen, thank you for keeping it real with me and staying on my ass. It paid off.

Capone, thank you for allowing me to reach out to you when I needed a helping hand.

C.J. Hudson, thank you for staying on me and making sure I got it done.

Thank you to my test readers, Aschandria, Virginia, Tonya, Cheryl and Shannon.

And to all my other LCB family members, I look forward to meeting and working with you because "we the best."

To my Myspace buddies who transitioned with me to Facebook, Cashae Russell (my sister of the pen), Niyah Moore (my pen twin), Allyson Deese and Chamsil. Y'all have been there from the beginning. We've had some fun going back and forth with our short stories and it's time for us to kick this game up a notch! Who's with me?

Shani Greene Dowdell, thank you for giving me the opportunity to showcase my erotic side in Mocha Chocolate 1 & 2. Thank you for all your support.

LaLaina Knowles, thank you for the opportunity to be a part of the Chocolat Historie D'Amour erotic anthology.

Kisha Green, I will keep an erotic story just for you whenever you're ready to do another anthology! Thank you for all your support.

I want to thank all of my social networking friends, especially Facebook, for supporting and believing in me. If I could thank you all personally, I would. You know who you are.

To Lisa Tyrell Perry, thank you for supporting this literary game like you do! You go hard for us! We appreciate it!

To Multiple Sclerosis (MS), thank you for making me stronger. I love a challenge and for fifteen years, you have given me one, but I always triumph!

To everyone who had me printing out my stories just so you could say you read one of mine, they're in book form now. I'm moving up thanks to you all for believing in me, pushing me, tooting my horn and stroking my ego.

To anyone that I forgot to mention, it wasn't intentional, but I thank you all from the bottom of my heart and deep down in my soul.

Last but not least, I want to give a shout out to my hometown, Prichard, Alabama. Just because I'm from a small town doesn't mean I can't do big things. P.A. all day, baby!

Smooches,
Carla

Chapter One

When we reached the ice and snack machines area, I grabbed Kingston's arm and yanked him from the hotel hallway. The force from my pull made him release his hold from our rolling luggage bags.

"What are you doing?" he laughed.

I said nothing as I pushed his six-foot-two frame between the ice and Coke machines. I then unzipped his pants and whipped out his dick.

Kingston looked around nervously. "Don't start something you can't finish."

I kept my eyes locked inside of his as I dropped to my knees and swallowed him whole.

"Ooooh, shit, Niquole," he moaned softly.

Instead of answering, I pretended like I was auditioning for a porno flick.

Sucking and slurping like next month's mortgage depended on my performance, I wasn't ready for our weekend to end. When I heard a light thump, I knew that his bald head had hit the wall. That let me know that I was doing a good job. My skills were even more confirmed when Kingston grabbed a wad of my hair and twisted it around in his hand.

"Honey, someone left their bags in the middle of…" an Asian woman stopped in mid sentence when she saw what was going down just a few feet away from her.

However, I wasn't about to stop. Pleasing my man was top priority. Besides, I knew Kingston wasn't going to let me. After watching the show for a few more seconds, she and her nearly same height, male companion kept on their merry way.

"They're gonna band us from the Clarion," Kinston said.

"Let 'em, we'll just find another hotel."

We preferred cheaper hotels. As crazy as it sounded, they provided more of a kinky sexual experience than the expensive ones.

"Bad girl. Mmmm, Niquole," he moaned and panted at the same time. "You know you've started something, right?"

I ignored him and continued at the task that was now in both my hands. When I felt his thrusts speed up, I knew that he was about to let loose, so I quickly pulled away.

"No, in me," I ordered, then hopped to my feet.

I eagerly pulled my skirt up and slid my panties to the side so that Kingston wouldn't have anything restricting him. Pressing me up against the wall, it wasn't long before I lifted one leg and waited for his manhood to glide inside of me. "Oh, Kingston…"

His thrusts were fast. I listened to him breathe heavily under my neck as I squeezed my pussy walls. He moaned and nibbled my neck each time I did so.

"Baby, you're about to make me cum doing that shit!"

I could care less that we were no longer behind closed doors, as I rolled my pussy all over his shaft. I couldn't let him leave me hanging. The friction from his chest to my breast caused my nipples to harden. My back slamming against the wall by the force of his deep, hard thrusts made a rhythmic beat that the producer, Timbaland could use on a track.

"Right there, baby! Right there!" I ordered and cheered as he hit the necessary spots to make me explode. "Faster…faster!" I was nearing my peak and knew it was going to be a good one as his speed increased. I loved it when we climaxed together. Moments later, we did just that.

"Baby," I breathed after Kingston finally pulled out. "I need to go back to the room and clean up a little," I continued, then slipped out of my underwear.

He reached inside his back pocket and gave me the room key. "I'll be out here waiting for you," Kingston breathed heavily. He bent over and rested his hands on his knees liked he'd just completed a marathon.

I smiled. "You need to be right behind me."

"For what?" he questioned.

I swept my forefinger across his dick, slipped it inside my mouth and sucked the juices off.

"Because I'm all over you, baby," I pointed at the mess between his legs. "You need to clean that up."

"I love the scent and sticky juices that you leave behind," he replied. "I need to get a drink after that stunt you just pulled," Kingston laughed as he retrieved some loose change from his khaki slacks.

"Get me one, too," I said before racing back to the room.

After opening the door, I smiled at the chaotic mess we'd left on the two double beds. I felt sympathetic toward the maroon and gold bedding because we'd tortured it with every ounce of strength in our bodies. It didn't stand a chance against our sex games.

I dashed to the bathroom, sat on the toilet and let the rest of me and Kingston's juices flow from my insides. Seconds later, I grabbed one of the white face towels to wipe the excess off the inside of my thighs then slipped back into my panties.

"Niquole, are you okay?" Kingston suddenly asked. "We gotta go before we miss our flights, baby," he rushed.

"I'm coming!" I yelled from the bathroom after flushing the toilet and washing my hands.

"Yeah, you did a lot of that, didn't you?" he teased. I

glanced in the mirror and smiled at his remark. "Niquole, baby, come on!" he rushed again.

"Okay…okay."

When I dried my hands and finally opened the door, my eyes widened when I saw him sitting on the bed stroking a fully erect dick. My heart pounded with each stroke his hand made.

"Don't we need to be getting to the airport?" I spoke before licking my lips.

He glanced at his diamond encrusted, Cartier watch then back up at me. "We've got time. Both of our flights don't leave until eleven. We got at least fifteen minutes to play."

I watched him moisten those luscious, LL Cool J lips with his thick tongue. Not only could I not say no to them, but fifteen minutes was more than enough time to bust a nut. Easing my red, satin panties down over my ass, I kicked them to the side as soon as they touched the floor.

"You should've just left them off," Kingston said with a wide grin.

"If I had known that we'd be doing this again then I would have."

Before he could respond, I gladly climbed on top of him. He grabbed a wad of my chestnut, brown locks that had fallen in the midst of all the intense heat we'd stirred up the night before. Kingston then jerked my head to the side so that he could latch his lips onto my neck. I could feel the tip of his dick beating against my stomach.

"He wants you," he whispered.

"I want him, too," I replied back before lifting my five-foot-four frame just enough for him to ease inside of me.

With much intensity, Kingston forced my black off-the-shoulder, Dior dress over my breasts and engulfed them. Whatever he wanted, I was prepared to give and whatever I wanted, I was prepared to take.

An hour and a half later, we collapsed on the bed.

"We need to call the airline and see what time the next flights are going out," Kingston spoke once our heavy panting died down.

I glanced at the clock on the night stand and laughed. Our original flights were long gone. He blew a long, deep sigh, sat up on the bed and retrieved his Blackberry Storm from his pocket.

"Who are you calling?" I asked after sitting up next to him.

I traced my tongue along his broad shoulders and the knife wound he said he'd sustained from a bar fight in his early twenties.

"I'm calling the airline. We need to get going," Kingston replied while dialing a number in his phone. "It's already 11:15 a.m. You know there's probably not another flight going out for a couple of hours."

"So, you just wanna linger around in the airport for a few hours like two terrorists?" I joked.

Kingston quickly placed his finger to his lips to hush me because a customer service representative had finally answered his call. While they went back and forth, I eased off of the bed and floated to the bathroom to freshen up again. This time, I decided to take a shower. After turning on the faucets and waiting for a comfortable water temperature, I stepped in front of the mirror and thought about me and Kingston's weekend. I was like a giddy, school girl smiling and blushing as I reminisced about us making love on the sink and on the toilet. I then noticed a few, light marks on my neck and knew they were from him latching on with his lips. Luckily, the marks weren't too noticeable against my light skin. I should've reprimanded Kingston for that shit because he knew how I felt about any evidence, but it was always hard to deny him especially when he worked his magic.

"They have a flight to Houston at 1:25. Mine doesn't leave until 2:00," Kingston startled me from the threshold of the bathroom door.

"Okay," I smiled from the mirror.

He stepped behind me and placed his hand on the sink. When I eased my fingers between his, I couldn't help but notice that our wedding rings were almost identical. At that moment, I wished that it was he and I who stood at the altar sliding the rings on each other's finger. *Why couldn't I have met you years ago?* I asked him silently when I gazed up at his reflection in the mirror. *You're perfect.* When he smiled back at me with those luscious lips and mysterious, dark eyes I wanted to melt.

"Come on, baby, we gotta get going. The planes aren't gonna wait for us," Kingston said, before tapping my ass then dashing back into the bedroom area.

I glanced at the steamy shower where I thought he and I would be making love again. It saddened me to know that we weren't.

"Come on, Niquole," Kingston commanded like he was my husband.

Little did he know, I wished he was the one who held that title.

Chapter Two

I sighed when the cab driver drove through the gates of my neatly manicured Houston subdivision nearly four hours after I was expected to arrive home. As I coasted through the neighborhood, I stared at each brick, single-family home and the families that were outside horsing around or tending to their yards. I wondered why I couldn't be that happy or why my mouth could never form a smile. The only time it did was when I was with him; Kingston. In the seven months that we'd known each other, he'd swept me off my feet and filled my world with nothing but excitement. Unlike my boring-ass marriage.

I wasn't ready to return to reality, but as the cabbie drove closer to my home, I had no other choice. I took a deep breath then reached inside my leather, Alma Louis Vuitton bag and pulled out a twenty dollar bill to pay the fare. When we pulled in front of the house, seconds later, I instantly frowned when I saw my mother's car in the driveway.

What the hell is she doing here, I thought. I certainly wasn't in the mood to deal with her ass at the moment.

However, my scowl instantly faded when I watched the enjoyment on my four-year-old son's face as he did cartwheels on the front lawn. When he spotted me, he made a mad dash toward the yellow cab. I gave him a huge smile as he patted on the window for me to hurry up and get out. I had to get myself together. I desperately had to jump back into my role as mother and wife. Even though I couldn't get Kingston off or out of my mind, I had to regroup for my boys' sake.

"Hey, Mommy!" Johnathan yelled. He jumped all over me when I stepped out of the cab.

I didn't show any painful emotion when he excitedly stepped on my foot.

"Whew, you smell like a wet dog." I playfully frowned as I gave him several kisses and hugs. "I see you got your hair cut," I said, rubbing my hand over his nearly bald head.

"Unhuh," he smiled with those perfect, beautiful, white teeth that I hoped would look the same once they fell out and the permanent ones came in.

"Where's your daddy?" I asked in a dry tone.

Before he could answer, I heard the front door open. As soon as I looked up, I saw my husband, Germaine, standing in the threshold of the door holding our five-month-old son, Nathan in his arms. I took a deep breath as I stared at him wishing, for a brief moment, he was Kingston, but I knew that he could never amount to my lover.

"Why are you so late?" Germaine asked as soon as I made it to the front door.

"Because I am," I replied in an irritable and defensive tone.

"Why didn't you call and tell me that you'd be late?"

"Because I didn't need to," I snarled. "Why all of the fucking questions? Damn!"

"I thought something may have happened to you Nikki...that's all. Besides, I left you four messages."

"I know," I replied nonchalantly.

"Well, why didn't you return any of them?"

"Germaine, are we really gonna do this now?" I huffed and pouted. I placed my right hand on my hip and shifted my weight to let him know that I wasn't in the mood. "I just got off the fucking plane."

When Germaine realized that he wasn't going to get any straight answers out of me, he dropped the whole interrogation.

"So, how was the trip?" he asked.

"Tiring."

If only he knew just how tiring it was. As my husband leaned down to kiss me, I turned my head slightly so that his kiss landed on my cheek. I, in turn, planted my lips on my bundle of joy's chubby cheeks. Germaine said nothing as I walked past him and into my 4,800 square foot house which, to my surprise, was still clean. Normally when I went out of town I came back to complete chaos…a bachelor's pad, but nothing could've upset me at that moment. I was still on cloud nine.

"You smell nice," Germaine complimented as he and Nathan joined me inside the house.

"Thanks," I replied dryly. "Where's my mother?"

He pointed toward the kitchen before continuing. "Is it new?"

"Why?" I asked then sucked my teeth.

"Because it doesn't smell like any of the other perfumes you wear."

Damn, does he pay that much attention to me? I thought. Kingston often told me that he loved the perfumes I wore, so I normally poured it on a little thick when we were together. "It's the new perfume by Beyonce'," I replied.

"Well, it smells nice."

I made a mental note to put it in the drawer until I was with Kingston again. I didn't want Germaine enjoying it. It was for Kingston's enjoyment only.

"I made reservations at seven o'clock at that hibachi restaurant that you and John John love so much," Germaine spoke as he rested his hands on my bare shoulders.

Using Johnathan was his way of getting me to say yes, but I wasn't in the mood to go out. I wanted to escape into my tub filled with hot, bubbly water to dream and reminisce about my time with Kingston.

"Let me ask you a question?" I addressed him. "How in the hell can you make reservations to a restaurant when you don't have any money?"

He gave me an uncomfortable look. "I thought maybe you wouldn't mind..."

"Spending my damn money?" I finished his statement. "You have a lot of fucking nerve. Isn't there something boxed in the freezer that you can throw in the microwave? Better yet, since you're *Mr. Mom*, can't you just throw some shit together like you've been doing?"

He gave me another uncomfortable look, cradled Nathan in his arms a little tighter and walked toward the door. "I'm happy you're home, Nikki," he replied before moping back outside.

As soon as Germaine closed the door, Johnathan ran inside. I didn't realize how filthy he was when he met me at the cab. His fairly new, gray and white Nike's were dingy and scuffed. Even his Sean John jean shorts and white t-shirt would need a miracle to come clean from the all the visible grass and dirt stains. I was more than sure that I'd be tossing those items in the trash. Germaine knew better than to let him play in those clothes, but I guess I was to blame for not being at home to supervise.

"Mommy, I'm getting my kickball. Daddy gon' kick with me," Johnathan spoke excitedly as he ran past me like the kid, Dash, from the animated movie *The Incredibles*.

"Okay," I said and smiled. "Have fun and don't hurt yourself."

As soon as Johnathan dashed upstairs to his room, I could hear him rummaging through his toy chest for his ball. At that moment, I rolled my Louis Vuitton suitcase through the tangerine colored living room, but stopped when I saw an ashtray filled with cigarette butts and two Bud Light bottles on the glass table. I was pissed. Germaine knew that smoking shit wasn't allowed in my house. I grabbed the filthy ashtray from the table and stormed outside. When he saw me with the evidence in my hand, he gave me a guilty and shameful look.

"Didn't I tell you not to smoke in the fucking house?" I growled at him.

"I know. I only did it when the boys were asleep."

"I don't give a shit if they're comatose! Don't smoke in here!" I yelled before throwing the ashtray at his feet causing some of the ashes to scatter. "If you find a fucking job then you won't have to smoke or drink!" I blasted before storming back inside the house.

Running into my mother didn't help the situation. I assumed she'd been ear hustling in the kitchen the entire time.

"Why do you treat him like that?" she asked before taking a bite into what appeared to be a peanut butter and jelly sandwich.

I stared into her hazel contacts and rolled my eyes. "Why are you even here?"

"Your husband called me over here to stay with the boys so he could go to the airport to find out what was going on with your flight. He was worried."

"Oh really. Well, there was nothing going on with the flight. I decided to take another one."

"Well, why would you do that and not let anyone know?" she asked.

I looked at my mother up and down because I knew she wasn't questioning me in such a way. Last I checked, I was no longer a child.

"Look, you can leave now," was my response. "As you can see, I'm fine."

It looked like she wanted to choke me. I knew that look all too well. *Jealous bitch*. She walked past me in her fitted, size six, Ann Taylor jeans, navy blue tank top and black flip flops. My mother was a forty-eight-year-old dime piece. She could wear anything and always made that shit look good. I was the same way and sadly, was also the spitting image of her.

"You're gonna lose a good man with that stank attitude of yours. You need to get your shit together, Nikki," she tried to chastise.

"Mind your own business and get out."

"Gladly."

As she walked out, I could hear her outside saying her goodbyes. Johnathan begged and whined for her not to leave, but she told him that she'd be back soon, then left.

I did everything in my power to not let anything that her or Germaine said get under my skin since I was on a feel-good high. But Germaine was pressing my nerves as usual. I knew he was going to be a softy when I first met him back in New Orleans six years ago. I was getting ready to burst onto the music scene with my sultry R&B sound while he assisted in producing tracks for my record. If only I'd known that my singing career would be shot to hell, I probably would've dropped his ass a long time ago.

Germaine was different from the other men that I'd dealt with in my past. He was supportive and I needed that boost. But as the days became weeks, the weeks into months and the months into years, I needed the aggression that I was beginning to miss and Kingston harpooning into my life gave me just that.

To avoid Germaine killing my mood, I disappeared behind the doors of my office where I spent the next few hours checking and replying to emails and messages that I received while out of town.

When I came out of my office nearly five hours later, I found Germaine on our chocolate, leather sofa in the living room with his feet kicked up. I couldn't believe his ass was watching *Tom & Jerry* on the Cartoon Network. Johnathan had fallen asleep in his lap and Nathan was in his arms.

"Don't you think you need to put them to bed?" I addressed.

He glanced up at me and stretched causing Johnathan to shift positions. "Are you done taking care of your business?"

"As done as I'm gonna be."

He yawned. "Good. Maybe you and I can have some alone time."

"If alone means me being in one room and you in another then that's fine with me. I don't know why you keep wasting your breath on that issue," I huffed before lifting Johnathan from his lap and carrying him to his room.

Although Johnathan smelled as though he'd been playing outside all day, I didn't bother removing his clothes. Germaine would just have to change and wash his covers when he did the laundry. By the time I slipped Johnathan's shoes off and covered his body with his favorite SpongeBob blanket, Germaine was on the other side of the room tucking Nathan in as well. I smiled as I watched Nathan's five-month-old body wiggle under the covers. I knew that he'd be waking up within the next few hours for a feeding, but that was going to be Germaine's job not mine. He carried his Mr. Mom title very well and I wasn't about to battle him for it.

After we put the boys to bed, I retreated to the kitchen to pour myself a glass of Moscato. I needed something to help shake Kingston out of my mind and to deal with the stresses of being back home. But something told me that Germaine wasn't going to let it be that simple.

"Did you get that guy on board?" he asked after following me into the kitchen.

I instantly frowned. "What?"

"Did you get that singer on board that you went to see in Tennessee?"

He'd caught me off guard. There was no artist. I'd used that excuse just to get to Kingston. Being the CEO of my own record label, *Kingquole Records,* gave me plenty of opportunities to see *my man*.

"He decided to go with a different label," I lied before sipping the wine.

"Oh, sorry to hear that. Well, your label is still doing well isn't it?"

"Yeah, my artists and staff are loyal to the label. Everything's good. In my eyes, it's slow, but I'm getting there."

"You talk like it's threatened," Germaine responded.

"No, it's not threatened. It's just that I expected it to be in a bigger place at this point in my life. I just need to push a little harder. Besides, I have a lot of big wigs backing me on it. I didn't go into this with my head in the sand."

"I didn't say that you did, but you knew that this type of business was risky."

"I do recall that you were once in this business, too," I seethed.

I was getting upset and he knew it. I didn't want to talk about my label not to him anyway. Germaine always seemed depressive when he would put his two cents in and I didn't need that.

"Germaine, I don't want to get into this with you now. Why are you pestering me? I know you want me to sit behind someone's desk, but that ain't me. I know you want me to come home at reasonable hours to help you with the boys, but my career is chaotic. You, of all people, should understand that."

"I do, Nikki. It's just that…"

"I can't sing anymore because of these damn nodules on my fucking vocal cords so it was only wise that I do something that involved music," I interrupted. I wasn't done with my speech. "You backed me on this when I first told you about it. So, I can't understand why you're tripping."

"I know I backed you. Hell, I was there when you were going through that shit. Remember? I've had your back since the beginning, so don't go there."

A few months before I was pregnant with Johnathan, I learned that I had nodules on my vocal cords which prevented me from singing. I was devastated. Since I was destined for great things, the drama hit me right after my first and last record was released. No matter how hard I tried, the surgeries I endured and defying doctor's orders, I knew that my singing career was over. It was heart-wrenching, but my passion for singing and music was so strong that I had no other choice but to start my own record label. Germaine didn't and couldn't understand that was one of the main reasons why I resented him. Kingston, on the other hand, understood the passion and drive.

Germaine interrupted my thoughts. "Nikki, will you please calm down."

I hated when he called me Nikki. "What do you mean calm down?" I barked. "I didn't work as hard as I have to back away now."

"I didn't say that you had to do any of that. Damn!"

"Then stop making me feel like I'm doing it for nothing. I'm doing what I love. Shit, this takes time. It's only been four years."

"If you know that it takes time then why do you keep bitching about it? I wanna be there for you, Nikki, but…"

"I didn't ask you to be," I interrupted then sighed trying not to get even more upset. "Look, everything is fine."

"How are we on money?"

I looked at him like he was crazy. Germaine knew I never discussed my financial situation with him. That information was strictly off limits. The most his ass had access to was a check card through our joint account. *Hell, if he knew just how much the label brought in on ring tones every month, he would be sick.*

"I'm not about to go into details with you about *my* money. Don't worry…we're not broke, so you'll still have money for alcohol."

Germaine shook his head. "It's always about *you,* ain't

it?"

"You're damn right! Why wouldn't it be? I'm the fucking bread winner in this house!"

"Well, if you build the studio like I asked, I could break back into the business and help out more around here."

"Are you serious?" I laughed heartily. "No one wants those whack ass tracks you make. I'm sure you're one of the reasons my album didn't go platinum."

I could tell that I'd crushed his heart, but still didn't give a damn. He needed to hear my truth.

"That shit was cold and unnecessary."

"It's the fucking truth and you know it. That's why you were ousted out of the business. You were like Ike Turner."

"What in the hell's that supposed to mean?" Germaine fumed. "I do recall that your album almost went platinum."

"Almost ain't fucking platinum," I barked before sipping the Moscato.

"I can always make a comeback, Nikki. I just need the right…"

"Person to give you the money," I finished his statement. "And you think that person is gonna be me?" I laughed again. "I don't think so. I'm taking care of the household and…"

"What are you trying to say?" Germaine interrupted in an extremely offensive tone. "Just because you make all the money now doesn't mean that I'm putting everything on you! I help out!"

"What do you think your weekly piece of shit unemployment check pays for in this house?" I taunted.

"I pull my weight around here, Nikki and you know it."

I had to give him that. He did his share. He bought food sometimes, diapers and things to maintain a household, but it wasn't enough for me. I wanted his ass to pay bills.

"Whatever, Germaine."

"All the money you spend on that unnecessary shit, you

could've easily built me a studio by now."

And tap into the secret account that I put aside for me and Kingston...please, I thought.

"Use the basement. You have enough bullshit down there anyway to start something."

Germaine bit his bottom lip as a show of defeat but, he wasn't done. "What about Johnathan?" he asked.

"What about him?"

"It was bad enough when you decided to take the guest bedroom and turn it into a huge fucking walk-in closet. As if the one in our bedroom wasn't sufficient. Then you took his room and turned it into an office when you already had one downstairs. Why do you need two? Johnathan needs his own room."

"You're truly killing my mood. Can we do this shit in the morning?"

"No, we're gonna do this shit now!" he screamed after slamming the palm of his hand against the butterscotch wall.

"I don't know who the hell you think you're screaming at," I snapped. "I'm not one of those skank-ass project bitches off the street."

"There you go again acting just like those project bitches that the fools on your label rap about!"

"What the fuck ever! I pay the mortgage on this damn house! I pay your car note! Do you think you would be driving an Escalade if it wasn't for me? I can do or say whatever the hell I want to in it!"

Germaine lowered his voice. "You need to give up Johnathan's bedroom, Nikki. The boys don't need to be in the same room anymore. Nathan wakes Johnathan up in the middle of the night and that's not good."

"And move back into the bedroom with you? Please," I laughed before sipping my wine again. "I'd rather sleep in the garage before I climb back into bed with your ass."

He had lost his mind. There was no way I was going to

give up my privacy. Besides, I turned Johnathan's room into an office just to be close to the master bedroom. During the nights Kingston and I had phone sex, I needed to hear Germaine's every move so he couldn't sneak up on me.

I began to stare at Germaine's green colored eyes that I once thought were sexy. He definitely reminded me of the actor, Michael Ely…minus the money. I'd lost all trust in him ever since he'd pulled the okedoke on me. If he hadn't been tampering with my birth control pills, Nathan wouldn't even be here and Johnathan would still have his own room. Nathan was an accident. The unexpected pregnancy was another reason why I resented my husband. I wasn't ready for another child and he deceived me into having one. Months were lost that could've been spent toward the label, and I blamed his ass for it all.

I took another sip of the Moscato and flipped my shoulder length hair before replying smartly. "I'm not giving up my office. If it's getting too crowded in their room, why don't you clean out the den, move into it and give Johnathan your room," I suggested sassily. "Better yet, build another room. Oh, that's right. You can't do that because you don't have a fucking job."

"Well, if you'd hire me on your label then I'd have one."

"You're in my pocket enough. I don't think you want to go even deeper, do you? But if I did offer you a job, how much do you think I'd pay you to clean the bathrooms?"

His nose flared instantly. I could tell that I'd stuck a knife through his heart, but I didn't care. There was no way I was going to have him moseying around my damn office finding out all of my secrets and shit. Besides, I saw enough of him at home. I didn't need him around me 24/7.

After my little smart remarks, Germaine started toward the door. He knew that walking away would piss me off.

"Where are you going?" I demanded. "You started this

shit."

"Started what?" he barked. "I asked you a simple-ass question and you blew it all out of proportion. I can't talk to you. I never can when you come home from these trips."

"Well, maybe you should stop talking then," I sassed.

"Nikki…"

"Will you please stop calling me Nikki?" I barked. "My name is Niquole!"

"It never seemed to bother you before," Germaine responded as if I'd crushed his heart yet again. "You used to like it when I called you Nikki."

"Well, it bothers me now. I'm not your fucking pet so drop the name."

"Whatever, Niquole Wright." He always had an issue that I didn't take his last name when we got married. My name meant the world to me and it eventually was gonna be household, so it was only wise that I kept my own last name.

"Don't get made because I didn't want Evans as my last name. Every time I think of that shit it reminds me of *Good Times*."

His chest rose and fell as he heaved his anger, but nothing that Germaine did would make his five-foot-eleven, well toned frame scare me. I watched his thick, eyebrows connect and his nose flare once again. His golden, honey skin darkened as if someone had lit a match under it. I knew that my words infuriated him, but as usual his bitch-ass said nothing.

Instead, he gave me a furious look, stormed out of the kitchen like a spoiled child, stomped up the stairs and slammed his bedroom door. Displaying an evil grin, I finished off the glass of wine and glanced at my purse that was lying on the counter. It took everything in me not to pull out my cell phone and call Kingston. I decided against it as I thought about Germaine's accusations.

I grabbed the bottle of wine from my LG, stainless steel, refrigerator, pulled one of the Venetian chairs from the round table and took a seat. I then poured myself another glass. Germaine was right. I always had an attitude when I came home from seeing Kingston. I guess I just didn't know how to control my emotions. I was always upset that I couldn't be with my lover and had to leave. I definitely needed to get my shit together.

After I finished my second glass, I walked upstairs to Germaine's bedroom when I heard him rustling around. Being nosey, I placed my ear against the door when I heard soft whispers. Pressing harder to see who he was talking to at this time of night, I quickly learned that he wasn't on the phone. He was praying. I listened to him begging and pleading to God to fix things between us. Stepping away from the door, I shook my head because his prayers were a lost...especially now that Kingston had entered the picture.

I retreated back into my office to check my emails and messages on my phone again before I called it a night. I swallowed hard when I came across an email that I dreaded opening. I clicked on the unknown sender and blew a long-winded sigh when I read it.

"I'm getting sick of this shit," I mumbled softly.

Two months after my affair began with Kingston, I started receiving emails from an unknown source threatening to expose my affair to Germaine. If I wasn't afraid that Germaine would take half if not all of my money, I wouldn't give a damn. I tabbed down to the end of the message and braced myself for the monetary amount the bastard would be asking for this time.

"Ten grand," I huffed. "That's the most they've ever asked for at one time."

I closed the laptop and set a reminder on my Blackberry to wire the money the next day. *The shit you have to do to keep secrets*, I thought

I hadn't spoken to Kingston in a little over a week. I was getting extremely pissed, irritated and agitated as each of my calls to him went straight to voicemail. Not hearing his voice and feeling his touch was driving me insane.

After pulling into an available parking space at my sons' daycare, Kingston must've been telepathically connected to me and felt what was going through my mind because he called. At this point, I was ready to use more of my frequent flyer miles to get to him.

"I need to see you," were the first words I heard when I answered.

I eased my silver, 2010 Lexus LS 460 in park, placed my hand between my legs and squeezed the inside of my thigh. I was hoping the pressure would control the urge for me to release all of those juices that had been stored since our last encounter.

"Niquole, are you there?"

"I'm here," I breathed. "I can be on a plane in the morning. Just tell me where I'm going." All my feelings about being pissed at him had quickly faded away.

"Meet me halfway…today."

"What are you talking about?" I giggled like an immature schoolgirl. "I can't meet you today."

"Yes, you can. It's a two and a half hour drive from

Houston and a two and a half hour drive from Dallas."

"What are you talking about, Kingston?" I giggled again eager to learn what was on his mind.

"Meet me in Waco?"

"You want me to drive to Waco?"

"Yeah. I've checked all the flights from Houston. Because of the nasty weather out here in Dallas, the next one isn't until later this evening. I just figured the drive to a halfway point would be easier and quicker. That's if you want to see me."

More than anything, I thought.

Instantly, I began to think back to when Kingston and I first met. I was eight months pregnant with Nathan and blown away at how much interest he showed me although I was carrying another man's child. I also didn't expect the affair to go that far, but it did. In my ninth month, I allowed Kingston between my legs. I knew I shouldn't have been on a plane so far along in my pregnancy, but Kingston was very convincing. I was happy that I thumped the angel of reason off my shoulder and joined Kingston in Miami. He rocked my world like no man had ever done before and at that moment, I knew I wanted him in my life forever. Whoever said pregnant sex was the bomb didn't lie because my orgasms were indescribable. He was the type of man that I needed on my team. Germaine's duration was over, but I had no other choice but to keep him around because I wasn't capable of juggling my career and a forced motherhood.

"Niquole, don't think too hard," Kingston said breaking my thoughts.

I glanced up at my sons' daycare center then looked at the numbers displayed on my car's dashboard clock. I was an hour early picking Johnathan and Nathan up for their doctor appointments. "I need to call Germaine to pick up the boys."

"Do what you need to do. I'm leaving in ten minutes and you need to be doing the same." I loved Kingston's take charge attitude. It turned me on deeply. "Homewood Suites on Legend Lake Parkway in three hours. Call me when you get there."

When he hung up the phone, I stared at the smiling faces of all the Disney characters on the daycare's front door. I wanted to bat my eyes like Minnie Mouse was doing to Mickey. I wanted to feel the happiness those characters were expressing and I knew Kingston could give me that feeling.

I pressed and held the number three button on my Blackberry until Germaine's throwback ring back tune *Love and Happiness* by Al Greene played. He picked up on the second ring.

"Hey," he greeted.

"Hey," I responded dryly. "Something came up and I need you to pick up the boys from daycare and take them for their doctor's appointment."

"Niquole, you told me you were getting them to do that," he spoke irritably.

"I know what I told you Germaine, but I need you to get them. Something came up."

"Something like what?"

"Look," I breathed heavily. "Can you stop asking so many damn questions? I just need you to get them. They don't need to miss this appointment."

"Niquole, I was on my way to the gym to get a few sets in before my interview today."

"So, is the fucking gym more important than you taking your sons for their checkups?" I asked harshly while pulling out of the parking lot knowing he wouldn't defy me.

"Don't do that. I'm not like you."

"Don't do what? If it wasn't for me, your membership to that bullshit ass gym would've been canceled months ago. And as far as that bullshit ass job you're trying to get, that's a fucking joke. A furniture salesman? Please." I laughed.

"Stop that shit, Nikki! I'm sick of you throwing your

money in my damn face. I'm trying to do the best I can to provide for my family."

"Then you need to get off your ass and get a *real* job so that I can stop wearing the pants in this family."

I heard the tires on his truck screech and horns in the background blowing. He obviously had slammed on brakes. "Damn it, Nikki! You're about to make me have a fucking accident! I'd have a fucking job if you'd bring me on with you!"

"Blah! Blah! Blah! Cry me a fucking river! Are you gonna get the boys or what?"

"I'll pick them up!" he screamed into the phone. "Your kids should be your priority not the damn label," he continued before ending the call.

Who says it's the label? I laughed internally.

I stared at the phone for a brief moment thinking about what Germaine said, but quickly threw his words out of my mind. Especially when thoughts of me being with Kingston appeared. If I didn't need Germaine to tend to our kids while I focused on my career, I would've left his ass a long time ago.

I pressed the number two button on my cell and listened for Lil' Wayne's *Drop The World* to ring in my ear. I would've given Kingston the number one spot, but it was voicemail use only.

"I'll be on the interstate in five minutes," I said when he answered.

"I'm already on it."

After we hung up, I called my assistant, Meagan and informed her that I wouldn't be in the office. I also told her to inform anyone who called that I would be in meetings all day. After that was done, I gassed up my car and hit the highway. I hadn't even been on the road five minutes before my cell phone rang again.

"Forget something?" I smiled into the phone, assuming it was Kingston.

"Hey, girl, what's up?"

I knew I should've looked at the caller ID before answering. "Nothing," I answered quickly hoping my friend, Jalisa, would pick up on the hint that I didn't have time to talk.

Jalisa and I had been friends since our middle school days back in New Orleans. She was the model and I was the singer. She stood five-feet-eleven-inches with legs for miles, size two waist, light brown eyes, silky black hair and a smile that would make you fall in love. She was beautiful and she knew it. When she told her parents that she wanted to be model, they immediately tossed her into the modeling world. She landed gig after gig while I sat back and sulked because my sorry ass mother wouldn't take me seriously when I told her I wanted to sing. I realized if I wanted it, I was going to have to get it myself and I did.

Jalisa and I parted ways when she landed a modeling contract in New York and I was getting my feet wet in the music business. However, when she learned that I and most of her family members had moved to Houston, she did the same. I thought that was a stupid move on her part. With the way her career was taking off, she should've stayed in New York or moved to L.A. We kept in touch, but it didn't matter to me if we did or didn't. I was always out for self and didn't need anyone hanging with me especially since she was a little pest. She was always trying to tell me right from wrong like I knew she was going to do if I engaged in a conversation with her.

"I'm a little busy, Jalisa. I'll have to talk to you later."

"Well, I was just letting you know that I should be home in…"

I cut her off. "Look, I'm going to meet Kingston. I'll call you later."

"I can't believe you're still seeing him," Jalisa chastised as she usually did. "You can't keep fooling around with…"

I hung up. I didn't have time for that nagging shit right now. Instead, I turned up my KEM CD to prepare myself for my man. I should've been ashamed of myself for driving nearly three hours to be with a man who wasn't my husband, but then again...I didn't care. If he'd asked me to drive five, just to be with him for thirty minutes, I would've done so. He was worth it.

I drove eighty miles per hour the whole way there with the wipers on full blast at times to deflect the bugs splashing against my window. I knew that the front bumper would be full of them when I stopped, so I made a mental note to run the car through a carwash when I made it back to Houston. The only reason I would use the gas station carwash was because I knew Bebo's or any other car detail shop would be closed by the time I made it back. Other than that, I wouldn't put my precious Lex through the carwash torture. Besides the bugs, I made sure to pay careful attention to the road and hidden, side pockets for any state troopers. I had loaned Meagan my radar detector when she decided to take a road trip a few weeks back and her ass hadn't bothered to return it. I was happy that there were no state troopers around because I could do without a ticket and the questions that Germaine would ask if he found out about it.

Exactly three hours later, I finally pulled up to the hotel. As I cruised the lot for an available space, it wasn't long before I spotted a jet black Navigator. I knew that it belonged to Kingston because those were the only SUVs he would rent.

"Baby, I'm here," I informed Kingston after parking and calling him on his cell.

After he gave me the room number, I stepped out of my car in my rainbow colored Juicy Couture tunic-dress and Marc Jacobs sunglasses hoping no one would recognize me or vice versa. Even though this was a low budget hotel, and most of my friends only stayed in five star establishments, I couldn't afford to be identified.

After sashaying through the lot and into the well-lit lobby, I smiled at the guests who spoke cordially. Luckily, no one recognized me. I was grateful because I didn't need anyone tweeting or updating their Facebook statuses, informing the world of my whereabouts. Basically, I didn't need Germaine finding out. On the other hand, I was pissed because of all the attention I used to receive during my singing years. *Boy I would do anything to get those times back.*

I walked past the lobby desk, returned the smile that the bubbly brunette gave me and headed for the elevators. The elevator wasn't going fast enough and all the people getting off on every floor made it even harder for me to get to my man. I was so anxious, I wanted to push them all off at one time. When the elevator finally stopped on the fourth floor, I quickly got off.

Left or right, I thought as I stared at the arrows pointing in the east and west directions of the rooms. Making a quick left, I skipped toward the room like a five year old. I even held back a laugh when walking past the snack machine. Thoughts of our last encounter crept through my mind and I wondered if we'd have the opportunity to christen that particular area.

When I made it to the room, the door was slightly ajar and I figured that Kingston had left it that way. I started to push it open, but stopped when I heard two male voices. My first thought was that he wanted us to do some kinky shit that I would quickly shut down and slap his ass for even suggesting it, but the conversation wasn't going in that direction. I jumped when the dark skinned, buff stranger stepped out. He smiled at me with his crooked teeth and walked away.

"What took you so long?" Kingston asked when I stepped inside the room.

I didn't say a word. I was too busy staring at his chest that bulged through his crisp, white Hanes t-shirt. I ignored his question when I felt a Kingston induced fever coming on. I sucked on my bottom lip and rubbed my foot on the back of my left calf. When Kingston noticed, he began to smile. He knew that I was getting hot and wasn't in the mood to waste any time with small talk. But I had to ask.

"Baby, who was that guy that just left?"

"He works at the bar downstairs. I asked him if he could bring up a bottle of Crown Royal, but I canceled the order," Kingston answered.

So, why is he in the room? I wondered, but quickly dismissed it as I watched him.

I saw the hunger and lust in his eyes as Kingston grabbed my hips and pulled me closer to him. When I felt his dick rise, I released a long awaited whimper. He disappeared under my neck while lifting my dress over my head. He then slipped his right hand inside of my lace panties and I began to tremble. My knees buckled and I felt wetness trickle down the inside of my thighs. I watched him drop to his knees, spread my legs apart and lick the juices. I was so happy for the mahogany dresser that was behind me because I needed something to catch me as I began to fall backward. My knees instantly gave out on me. I leaned my head back on the glass mirror as he grabbed my legs, threw them over his shoulders and disappeared between them. I closed my eyes and enjoyed my version of heaven.

"Mmmmm," Kingston moaned. "I think this pussy got sweeter after you had your son."

My trip to heaven was interrupted when I felt my body rise from the dresser. Kingston reached behind my back and unsnapped my bra while I pulled his t-shirt over his head. I watched him smile when I began to take control and pushed him onto the bed.

"Take what you want, baby," he spoke as I unbuttoned, unzipped and eased his cargo shorts down his leg. I'd prepared myself to drop and give him fifty. He immediately kicked off his navy and white canvas shoes when he saw where my mouth was headed. "Shit, Niquole," Kingston said when his dick disappeared inside my mouth.

Suddenly, he began to claw and pull at the sheets as I careful licked each one of his balls. Obviously unable to take my skills, he threw his head back and covered his face with a pillow. He even yelled out a bit. At that moment, I felt the throbbing between my legs so I reached for my wet pussy and went to town. My fingers helped to scratch my itch, but I needed him inside of me. The foreplay had gone on long enough.

When I attempted to climb on top of him, Kingston stopped me. Helping me off of the bed, we stood face to face before he placed his hands atop my shoulders, pressed me to my knees and guided his dick back inside my mouth. Pulling out his thug card, he then grabbed a wad of my hair.

We both rocked back and forth. I often tried to take all of him inside my mouth, but the gag reflex was a sure sign that I couldn't. Ever since the first time I went down on him, Kingston was determined to have my lips touch the base of his dick. As much as I wanted to, I couldn't allow him that pleasure for fear that I'd vomit. However, I clasped both of my hands around his thickness so that he would stop pressing the issue. Minutes later, he pulled out and we watched his babies ooze between my breasts. Before I stood up, I made sure that he was erect again, then I shoved him back onto the bed.

"Now, it's my turn to get what I want," I said.

"It's yours for the taking, Niquole. Do you," Kingston replied then placed his hands behind his head and waited for me to start.

I climbed on top with my back facing him and planted my feet firmly on the bed before I began my ride. I knew that he wouldn't be able to withstand and resist the pleasurable torture. His hands soon came unglued from behind his head. I held onto his legs while he gripped, clawed and squeezed my back.

"Damn, baby," Kingston moaned, as he tried to keep up with the speed of my bounce. "I like it when you take control!"

I leaned over a little further and rose up a tad to tease him. But he wasn't going for that. Instead, he gripped my hips and forcefully jerked my body back and forth. I hoped no one thought that I was being raped by the screams that flew out of my mouth. Moments later, he flipped me onto my back. I loved it when he man handled me that way, and he knew it.

"My turn," Kingston growled.

He stood up in the bed, grabbed my legs and pulled me to him. I had no other choice but to take all ten inches of him. Now, it was my turn to yell into the pillow. Seconds later, the bed started knocking against the wall as it usually did when we were together. I couldn't control myself, nor could he. We both yelled and screamed to the top of our lungs as sweat beaded up on our faces and dripped like a faucet. I reached for whatever I could grab. When my hand landed on the lamp cord, I pulled it as Kingston continued hitting all of my spots. It immediately fell onto the floor, shattering the bulb. However, that didn't stop my man. He released my legs, but they remained over his shoulders. He then placed his hands on the wall for leverage.

"Kingston! Oh my God!"

Of course, my cries went unanswered. When I opened my eyes, he was staring into mine like a true lover. We continued to gaze at each other until suddenly, I heard something click. I took my eyes off of Kingston and motioned them above my head, right before I saw the headboard coming toward us. Instantly, Kingston pulled me to safety before it had a chance to land on my face. After asking if I was okay, we both laughed, but that didn't stop us.

Somehow, we ended up on the floor. I knew that I was going to have some serious carpet burns on my mulatto skin, but I didn't give a damn. Once again, our eyes and lips locked and our sweat mixed. Twenty minutes later, we both reached our climax and finally collapsed. Desperately trying to catch our breath, we didn't say a word for at least ten minutes. When I finally turned to him, we burst into laughter again.

"You're paying for the head board," I said.

I laid my head on his dark chocolate chest and began twirling his curly chest hairs between my fingers. He eased his body from underneath me and went to inspect the headboard. I thought he'd picked an awkward time to do it especially since we were cuddling. Well, at least that's what I wanted to do.

"Did I tell you that I got the papers about the name change for the label?" I tried to make small talk as I pulled myself from the floor and sat on the bed.

"Yeah, you did. What did your boy, Germaine have to say about it?"

"He asked me why I changed it and where did I get the name from?"

"And what did you tell him?" Kingston asked nonchalantly.

"I told him that the label was my king since it was paying bills and I used the last part of my name."

"And he bought that shit?"

"I don't know and I really don't care. Besides, I told you how gullible he was. He believes everything I tell him."

Instead of replying, Kingston seemed to be pretty occupied trying to place the headboard back on the wall. It bothered me, a little, that he wasn't too enthused about me changing my label to include his name. Kinquole Records didn't sound as good as Bossy, but I wanted my man to be a part of my empire.

"Do you remember when we first met?" I asked, changing the subject hoping that would draw his attention.

"How can I ever forget?" he laughed. "You were going off on the people at the Dallas airport for losing one of your bags."

"Skip that part," I giggled.

"I helped you locate your bag and the rest is history," Kingston said as he finally turned to me and smiled.

I had his attention again.

"Do you remember how many times you made me cum when we first had sex?" I asked.

"Yeah, I remember. I also remember that you went into labor a day after that."

I smiled naughtily. "That was your fault."

"I'll take the blame."

"I wish you lived in Houston, Kingston. Things would be so much simpler."

Before we could go any further into the conversation, there was a knock on the door. Not sure who it was, I yanked the sheet off the bed, and wrapped my body in it while Kingston slipped on his gray boxer briefs that cupped his tight ass and thighs so well. I wanted him to turn around so that I could see how his dick fit in the front. At that moment, he must've read my mind because he did just that. His dick looked like a four hundred pound man squeezed inside of a Mini Cooper. Yeah, he was packing like that.

I was a little uneasy as I watched Kingston walk to the door as if he was expecting someone. He then opened the door just enough to retrieve the slip of paper the person was handing him. The entire thing seemed strange as I maneuvered my head to see if I could catch a glimpse of the person. Even though I couldn't see that well, I did manage to see the person's shirt. It was the guy Kingston was talking to when I first came in.

"What did he want?" I asked when Kingston closed the door and walked over to the floor where his pants were.

He pulled out his wallet. "He wanted to give me the receipt for the Crown Royal that I ordered earlier."

That's funny...I thought you cancelled that order, I thought. I quickly wondered why he felt the need to lie to me.

Chapter Four

"Nikki, we need to hurry up so we can drop the boys off. I don't want to be late," Germaine rushed me the following Saturday night.

We'd been invited to one of his Omega Psi Phi frat brother's parties; a party that I didn't want to go to, but he practically begged me to attend. I'd never met any of his frat brothers before and didn't want to. What was the fucking purpose anyway? They would probably try to woo me away from his weak-ass anyway. Besides, he hardly ever talked about them, so I assumed they were not really important to him. Thinking back to my years at Louisiana State University and all the frat parties I attended, I cringed at the thought of hearing *Who Let the Dogs Out* or *Atomic Dog* all night long. I could've found better things to do with my time than watch some, sweaty frat brothers relive their golden, college years stomping, stepping and woofing all night.

"Nikki, are you almost done?" Germaine yelled from down the hall. I was purposely taking my time in hopes that he would leave me behind to avoid the ghetto madness that I was going to walk into. "Nikki, please hurry up!" I knew the only thing that would get me through the night was thinking about my rendezvous with Kingston just three days earlier. "Nikki!" Germaine continued to yell.

"I'm coming! Shit!" I finally yelled back.

I took one last look at myself in the dark cherry, Cheval oval mirror. I couldn't help but agree with the blog posts, comments as well as a few employees at the label who said I looked like a lighter version of Kerry Washington. We even shared the same full perky lips. Of course, I looked better though.

I knew those bitches at the party wouldn't stand a chance against my size five frame. I was flawless with my strapless Versace dress, Christian Louboutin shoes and diamond studs that gleamed in my ears. I was the shit and I knew it. After blowing myself a kiss in the mirror with my nude colored lips, I walked out of my office and down the hall.

"You're rushing me and you don't even have the boys' bags," I huffed at Germaine. I tried my best to pick an argument so that I could use that as an excuse to stay home.

"The bags are in the car with the boys," he replied.

"You left the boys outside alone?"

"The boys are fine, Nikki. I just put them in the car. I didn't even start it yet," Germaine said as he dangled the keys in my face. "Can we please just go?"

"You're acting like a giddy teen on prom night. What's up with that?"

"Listen, I know what you're trying to do."

"What are you talking about?" I questioned.

"You're trying to get out of not going, and that's not fair. I'm always by your side at any function that you attend or have."

That's just it, you're not the one who I want by my side, I thought. "Can we just go and get this shit over with," I replied, clutching my handbag under my arm.

"Look, don't do me any fucking favors!" Germaine snarled at me. He then stomped out the door and slammed it behind him.

It bothered me when he acted like a whiny bitch on her period. I thought it was funny. *What real man acts in such a way*? As I was about to open the door and curse his ass out, my mother called.

"Yeah?" I irritably answered my phone.

"Well, damn, I was just calling to check on the boys."

"They're fine. We're about to take them to Germaine's mother's house."

"For what?"

"If you must know, I'm going to a crappy ass party with Germaine and his mom is keeping the boys."

"Why didn't you ask me to keep them?"

"I don't fucking know!" I answered impatiently. "Ask Germaine. He calls you for everything else!"

I ended the call quickly before she had a chance to crawl under my skin. Besides, I had other matters to tend to. Germaine wasn't off the hook since he wanted to grow some balls a few minutes ago. He knew better than to yell at me. I swung the front door open with an attitude. "What the hell was that?" I barked after catching up to him.

"I'm not letting you ruin my night, Nikki."

"I'm not trying to ruin your damn *frat* night," I stressed. "Why is this party so fucking important to you anyway?"

"It's not just the party, Nikki. Besides wanting to see some of my old buddies that I haven't seen in a while, it's about you, too."

I crinkled my freshly arched eyebrows. "I don't understand."

"I would love to flaunt my sexy, successful wife on my arm sometimes instead of the other way around."

I don't flaunt you, fool, was what I wanted to say but I settled for, "I'm sure you would," I mumbled.

"What'd you say?"

"Nothing, Germaine," I replied before climbing in the passenger seat. I kept quiet the entire drive to his parents' house.

When we arrived twenty minutes later, I glanced in the backseat at my boys and saw that they'd both fallen asleep. I giggled as I watched my four-year-old's thumb dangle from his mouth and the five-month-old's pacifier hang from his.

"Are you gonna help me with the boys and their stuff?" Germaine asked after turning off the ignition.

"You can handle it," I replied after restarting the car and turning the AC up a few degrees. The nightly June humidity was making me sweat and I couldn't have that.

"Don't you at least wanna say hello to my folks?"

"Now, why in the fuck would I want to do that, Germaine?" I asked nastily. "They don't give a shit about me and the feeling is mutual."

"I just thought maybe…"

"Germaine, take the boys inside and let's go!"

He shook his head at me then climbed out of the car. It took him two trips to carry the sleeping boys and their things up and down the six steps that led to the front door of the house. Seconds later, I saw his fat, wig wearing mother peep out the door on his second trip. I knew that she didn't want to, but for her son's sake, she slightly waved at me. I threw my hand up then turned my head in a different direction so that I wouldn't have to look at the bitch a second longer. I didn't care for her ass after I overheard her talking shit about me to one of her friends before Germaine and I got hitched. She told her friend that I didn't deserve her son. *Who was she to say those things about me although every word that she spoke was the truth?* I watched her remove Nathan from Germaine's arms and gently place him over her shoulder before hugging her son goodbye. Afterwards, he raced back down the steps and into the car.

"Can you kick that dirt off of your shoes before you get

back in *my* car?" I asked as he was about to plant his white Airforce Ones on my newly acquired custom made Kingquole Records printed rugs.

Germaine sighed heavily, but did as he was advised. "Anything else, Queen?" he asked sarcastically.

"Don't tempt me," I sassed back.

"Okay, Nikki. You win."

Always do. "I thought I told you to stop calling me Nikki."

"I've been calling you Nikki for years so I'm not about to stop now," he snarled before jerking the car in reverse.

I huffed and frowned at his attire that consisted of jeans, a polo style shirt and of course the same tennis shoes he wore every fucking where. While I looked like a million bucks, he was dressed like something off of a Wal-Mart clearance rack. He used to dress in nice clothes when we first met, but soon stopped. His reasoning was that he didn't have to impress anyone and was comfortable with his new look. Well, I wasn't. Like oil and water, we didn't mix and that added even more bitterness toward him.

We didn't talk the entire twenty-five minute drive to the House of Purple on Commerce Street. I made sure that my Usher CD was loud enough to drown out any conversation that he may have wanted to start. I knew Germaine wouldn't say anything to me for fear that I'd want to argue and ruin his night, which I was surely capable of doing.

We pulled into the parking lot of the fraternity hall and into an open parking spot.

"Are we okay?" Germaine asked. He turned to me and placed his hand on top of mine. I slightly laughed before pulling my hand away.

You may be, but I'm not was what I wanted to say, but I settled for a simple "I'm straight. Let's just get this over with."

As soon as he stepped out of the car in his old ass

Rockawear jeans, Germaine was attacked by a kennel of his dogs. For over five minutes, I watched them hug, shake hands and laugh as if they were long lost buddies. In that brief moment, he'd forgotten all about me. I was furious because, no matter good or bad, I had to have all the attention.

Pushing my door open, I stepped out, walked around to his side of the car and coughed to make my presence known. The looks on the boys' faces when they saw me said that they knew he was a lucky man.

"Everybody, this is my beautiful wife Nikki…I mean Niquole," Germaine said as he placed his arm around my waist. I tried to step away, but he pinched my arm for me to stay put.

"Hi," I addressed them all after they personally introduced themselves to me.

"Germaine, my man, where have you been hiding this one for all these years?" someone yelled out.

"*This one*?" I repeated.

"Hummer, don't start, man," Germaine intervened before I could let loose on him. "Nikki is a very busy woman."

"When you run your own business, you don't have time for little people," I interjected.

I could tell that I'd struck a nerve. All of them turned to Germaine who tried to hide the stunned look on his face.

Another one of the frat brothers tried to break the ice. "So, what is it like being a big time record producer?"

The others stared at me waiting for my answer. "I'm not a record producer. I *own* my record label. There's a difference," I stressed then flashed my pearly whites.

"So, when can we stop by the studio and…" a stout, pimple faced frat brother began.

"Boys," I interrupted with a bright smile as I seductively clutched Germaine's arm, "It's playtime and I don't talk business when I'm playing."

They all laughed. "We'll see ya' inside," one of them

addressed Germaine as they walked toward the hall.

"What in the hell was that?" Germaine asked after pulling away from me with a pissed off look on his face.

"That was for leaving me in the fucking car. Besides, I thought you wanted me to be *friendly*."

"Why can't you behave?" he heaved. "You're a piece of work, Nikki. I guess you lied to me when you told me that we were okay."

"I didn't say that *we* were okay. I said that *I* was straight," I corrected him.

"For once in your life, can you give a damn about someone other than yourself?" Germaine said before stomping away.

He left me standing in the slightly dark parking lot and jetted inside the hall. I shrugged my shoulders then laughed at his childish move. Instead of following him inside, I hopped back in the passenger seat of the car, pulled out my cell phone from my purse then pressed #2…the speed dial for Kingston's number. No answer. I waited five minutes before trying again. Again, no answer. After letting out a huge sigh, I dropped the phone back into my purse, hopped out of the car and headed for the hall. When I made it to the door, I bumped into Germaine.

"Nikki, I'm sorry for flipping out like that. I was just on my way out to get you," he said trying to hand me a Corona.

"I'll bet you were." I rolled my eyes then attempted to walk past him, but he gently grabbed my arm.

"Nikki, please don't do this tonight," he begged. "This is an important night for me."

I glanced around the room at all of his fraternity brothers who were having fun, drinking, telling jokes, reminiscing and dancing. At that moment, I decided not to ruin Germaine's night. I figured we wouldn't be together much anyway so there was no point in doing so. When he saw that I was easing up, he tried to hand me the Corona again.

"Just because I'm in the hood, doesn't mean I have to act hood," I said, turning my nose up at the beer.

"You're not in the hood," Germaine corrected. "You used to drink Coronas when we lived in Louisiana," he reminded. "Besides, snooty people drink beer, too."

"Snooty?" I laughed. "I don't want the fucking beer, Germaine. Just because you still drink them doesn't mean I have to."

"Look, we won't be here long. I promise."

"I hope I don't have to deal with this shit all night," I said watching the men make complete asses of themselves. They were posted up on all fours acting like a dog and centipede on the floor in their purple or gold shirts.

"Just be nice. We won't be here all night."

"I hope the hell not," I mumbled before walking off.

Chapter Five

As I walked the room, I noticed all the men and women staring at me. Hell, I couldn't blame them though. They saw confidence, attitude and money and knew that Germaine had picked a good one. The women wanted to be in the size five dress that I was rocking and the men wanted to be under it. I knew that I was going to be overdressed when I picked out my outfit, but that was my point. I wanted all eyes on me. Again, I loved attention whether it was bad or good.

I walked over to the open bar that was made up of two long, buffet tables. Those crowding the tables helped themselves to beer from kegs, bottles of Hennessey, Courvoisier or whatever was available. I wanted a glass of champagne, but quickly realized I wasn't going to get one after seeing all the ghetto, red cups being passed around.

"Amateurs," I pouted softly.

Suddenly, the DJ began playing the *Cupid Shuffle.* I was nearly trampled over as everyone made a mad dash to the dance floor like it had rained EBT cards with the pin numbers.

"You wanna go out there?" someone asked.

I turned around, and was faced with one of Germaine's frat buddies from outside. I wondered if someone told him that the Mohawk style didn't look good on his lemon shaped head.

"You're Hummer, right?" I asked trying to remember the names during Germaine's introduction. I stepped away from him because he was all over my dress.

"Yeah, I'm Hummer," he answered with drunken eyes and alcohol breath.

"What kind of name is Hummer?"

"Ask about half of these women in here," he slurred. "I hum on that pussy and…"

"T-M-I! I don't need nor do I want to hear that," I replied then turned my nose up at him.

"Alright then," he laughed. "So, you don't shuffle?"

"Absolutely not. Nor do I swag surf, stanky leg, booty do, crank that or jerk."

"What?" he asked.

"In simple terms that you may understand, I don't dance."

"Do you think you're too good to do the hood dances?"

I smiled. "Are you serious? I'm from the hood and besides, I have rappers on my label so don't come at me with that shit."

"Then what's the problem?"

"I just don't fucking dance," I snapped.

"Then you can't be from the hood," Hummer responded.

"Let me explain something to you, sweetie. I'm from the hood, but I'm not hood. And one thing has nothing to do with the other. You understand?"

"Someone as sexy as you and with an ass like yours should be out there flaunting her stuff," he slurred. I was beginning to feel a little uneasy, but I held my composure. "Germaine won't mind if that's what you think."

Something about his statement instantly bothered me. "He probably won't mind, but I do. What is that supposed to mean anyway?"

"So, I guess Germaine never told you about how we used to share, huh?" Hummer spoke as he pressed against me. I instantly shoved him off of me before he could scuff my shoes.

"What the fuck is your problem?" I barked at him.

He grabbed me by the arm when I tried to walk away. "I…I'm sorry," he apologized. "I didn't mean anything by what I said," he stated. "I just had too much to drink tonight."

I yanked my arm away and searched for Germaine through the purple, gold and white balloons that were floating everywhere. Seconds later, I spotted him at a table conversing with a few of his friends. I walked up with an instant attitude.

"Hey, baby. This is Tyrell," Germaine introduced. "He's the one who I told you about. You know…the one who's getting married."

"I'm ready to go," I spoke frantically, ignoring his introduction as well as Tyrell's fat hand that was extended.

Germaine could see the disturbed look on my face and hopped out of his seat. "What's wrong? What happened?"

"We need to go, Germaine. I can't stay here in this shit- hole."

I could tell by his friend's faces that they were a little bothered by my remark, but I didn't care.

"Nikki, just thirty more minutes," Germaine pleaded in a whisper.

"Fine. Find your own damn ride home," I snarled after snatching the keys off the table next to his Newports and black lighter.

I pushed through the crowd, stomped out of the hall and toward the car pointing and pressing the key to unlock the door.

"Are you okay?"

When I turned to the voice, I revealed a startled look on my face.

"I didn't mean to scare you. You and Germaine alright?"

It was Hummer.

"That's none of your fucking business. I told you to

leave me alone." When I opened the driver's door, he slammed it shut. "What the fuck are you doing?" I stared into his beady eyes. I then glanced at the hall and realized that the distance from the car to the front door was too far to run in the four and a half inch heels I had on. "G…Germaine should be out here any second," I stuttered.

"Well, until he comes, I think we can find something to do," Hummer replied as he backed me against the car with his body.

"Get the hell off of me!" I spoke loudly, hoping some-one would hear me over the loud music inside. I squeezed the keys inside my right hand and whacked him across the head with them. At that point, Hummer staggered backward and grabbed his head to see if he was bleeding.

"You stupid bitch!" He charged at me forcing my body against the car. I fought with all my might to break free, but he was too strong. "Bitch, I told you that me and Germaine shared." I turned my face away from him after smelling his al-cohol scented breath when he tried to kiss me. "Don't fight this, bitch," Hummer continued as he reached under my dress and into my panties. "I feel the heat coming off of this pussy baby. Just the way I like it," he said, sounding like a horny per-vert.

I clenched my thighs together when he tried to force his fingers inside my goodie jar. But before Hummer could win that battle, he was yanked away.

"Nigga, have you have lost your fucking mind!" Ger-maine barked before shoving Hummer on the ground.

Furious, I ran around Germaine and kicked Hummer in the face as hard as I could then stomped the heel of my shoe in his chest. When he removed his hand from his mouth, I saw that he was bleeding. I went to kick him again, but Germaine grabbed me.

"Hummer, this is some fucked up shit, man and you know it!"

"I thought we were boys, G," Hummer addressed Germaine when he picked himself up off the ground. "It used to be what was yours was mine and what was mine was yours."

"Nigga, that was fucking college! This is my wife! You need to get the fuck away from me before I hurt you." Hummer took heed to Germaine's threat and walked away with his tail between his legs. "Did he hurt you?" Germaine questioned as he looked me over and caressed my face.

I instantly slapped his hands away. "Is that it?"

"Is what it?"

"He just attacked me and you're just gonna let his ass go?"

"Nikki, he's drunk!"

"Drunk or not, he just tried to rape me! Did you not see where he had his hand? In my pussy, Germaine! In my pussy! I did more to him than you did!"

"Look, calm down."

I couldn't believe what I was witnessing or hearing. *Was he really gonna let this mofo get away with almost raping me?* He needed to know this was unacceptable.

"I will not calm down. If you hadn't brought your ass out here that nigga would've raped me, Germaine!" I screamed after shifting my weight to one side to let him know that I was really pissed.

"Nikki, he's drunk. I'm sure he didn't mean any harm," Germaine attempted to convince me.

"You're a fucking idiot! No real man would let that asshole get away with that shit!"

"Let's just go home and cool down."

I watched my husband glance back and forth and side to side to see if anyone was witnessing our argument. I knew that causing a scene was making him a bit uncomfortable, but as usual I didn't care. He needed to know just how uncomfortable I felt. I glared at him with my light brown eyes. If looks could kill, he'd be dead. He pulled his pack of Newports from his back pocket. But before he could slide one out of the pack, I slapped it out of his hand. Immediately, those thick, black eyebrows of his connected and his nose flared.

"So, you wanna hit me over some fucking cigarettes and not that nigga who just tried to rape me?" I taunted.

"Fuck this!" Germaine yelled while throwing his hands up in the air. "The damn man is drunk! Hummer could never hurt a soul!"

"What did you two do in college?" I asked.

"What? What are you talking about?" he asked dumbfounded.

"That asshole, Hummer, told me that you used to *share everything*. What the hell was he talking about?"

When Germaine started scratching his head, I knew that I'd struck a nerve. "It was nothing, Let's just go home."

"No. You shared women, didn't you?"

He sighed. "Listen, it was just once, but the girl was willing. She liked both of us anyway."

"I knew there was a reason I didn't wanna come here tonight," I rolled my eyes at him. "Take me home. Now!"

"Nikki, I'm sorry."

"Fuck that sorry shit! You don't have to worry about me attending anymore of these fucking parties."

I climbed into the passenger seat and waited for him to hop behind the wheel. I then peeped out the corner of my eye and watched him lean against the car and place his face in his hands. It looked as if he was trying to figure out a way to fix things between us. But there was nothing he could do and I think he knew that. "Germaine," I called out to him as I leaned over and tapped on the window to get his attention, "let's go."

The ride home was an exact duplicate of the ride there…quiet. All I could think about was my husband not defending my honor in the way he should have and I knew he was thinking the same. *What would Kingston have done if someone had assaulted me?* I thought.

As we hopped on I-10, I couldn't help but notice all of the hotels as we passed by. I wished I was locked behind one of the doors with my lover instead of riding home with my weak ass husband. He was beginning to disgust and annoy me even more and I think he had a clue of this as well.

When we arrived home, I hopped out of the car before he could put it in park then dashed inside the house. Germaine soon followed, grabbing me before I could disappear into my hideaway. I yanked away.

"Don't fucking touch me!"

"Wow! Where'd that come from?"

I gave him a disgusted look. "Where the fuck do you think? You should've kicked his ass!"

"What would that have solved, Nikki? Would it have made you feel better if I had gave his ass a busted lip, a black eye or maybe a bloody nose?"

"Yes," I answered sternly.

"I'm not a violent man and you know that. You shouldn't expect violence from me."

"Violence has nothing to do with this situation. What if you hadn't come outside? What if it had gone further than it did?"

"That's different."

"No, it's not because your weak ass wouldn't have done anything more than…"

I stopped in mid sentence when I watched Germaine turn into the Incredible Hulk and punch a hole in the wall. "Is that what you want? Is that what you wanted me to do to him? It's over! You don't have to worry about him!" he screamed. "I don't want to talk about this shit anymore! It's done! It's over with!" he growled then stepped in my face.

My smart mouth couldn't produce any words and at that particular moment I don't think I even wanted to. He brushed past me with an angry, yet hurt look on his face, stomped to the bedroom and slammed the door. As bad as the situation had turned out, I wasn't gonna spend the rest of my evening worrying about him or his feelings. Instead, I trotted to the kitchen, and poured myself a glass of Moscato. I needed something to relax me after the night's events.

After walking into the living room and taking a few sips from my glass, I heard the upstairs shower in the master bedroom running. At the same time, I heard my cell phone ringing inside my purse. I glanced at my watch. I knew that it could only be Kingston calling me at one a.m., and luckily Germaine wasn't around to question me about it. I placed the glass on the coffee table and anxiously dug around in my purse for my phone.

"Hello?" I answered.

"I see you called. What's going on?" Kingston spoke.

"Tonight was fucked up, Kingston. It was really fucked up," I breathed and sighed into the phone while tiptoeing to my office downstairs.

"I'm listening."

I spent the next ten minutes telling him about the night while Germaine obviously took a long ass shower like a bitch.

"Germaine is a weak nigga, Niquole," Kingston said after he heard the story. "He has no fucking balls. He should've got all up in that nigga's shit."

His words were so intense and extremely passionate, I hung off of every one of them.

"I know, but it's over now. I told him that I'm..."

"It's not over until I say it's over," Kingston interrupted before disconnecting the call.

Chapter Six

"I can't wait 'til I'm in your arms again and feel your hands all over my skin," I sang in the shower while reminiscing about my last performance on stage. I remembered it like it was yesterday although it was nearly six years ago. The Hard Rock Café in New Orleans had sold out all because of me. The first single, *Love Under Me*, and only album, *Things Change*, went gold in less than a week. I was a force to be reckoned with and everyone knew it. However, I was devastated when that spotlight was turned off. Now, singing in the shower was my new stage. *"Your breath against my neck sends chills up and down my spine..."*

I stopped singing when Germaine startled me by barging into the bathroom screaming about my vibrating phone. I grabbed one of the thick, green towels from the rack, wrapped it around my wet body and snatched my phone from his hand.

"Why in the fuck are you going through my damn phone?" I demanded while scrolling through it to see the calls and texts that I'd missed.

I swallowed hard when I saw they were all from Kingston. Thankfully, I had given him a nickname. *Mercy.* That was the name of one of the artists I wanted to sign to my label, but he chose to go elsewhere. Little did he know, his name still came in handy.

"I...I didn't go through your phone," Germaine stuttered curiously. “Is there a reason I should’ve?

“I just don’t want you snooping through my things.”

“Again, is there a reason I should? You’re my wife. I’m your husband. We don’t have secrets. Right?”

You may not have any, but I have a slew of them. “Can you leave me alone so that I can get dressed?”

Germaine gave me an uneasy and unpleasant stare as he walked out of the bathroom. I cursed myself for leaving my phone on the kitchen table in the first place. I was never that careless. After he left, I hurried to the door and locked it. I was eager to talk to Kingston because it had been a week since I last spoke with him. I pressed the number two key on my phone and waited anxiously for him to pick up.

“Why in the hell are you not answering my texts or calls?” Kingston demanded as soon as he answered.

“Well…” I started before he interrupted me.

“There’s a wrecker service on Brittmore Road. Be there within the hour.”

While Kingston was talking, Germaine was yelling something to me through the bathroom door. I ignored him to focus on Kingston’s words instead.

“Wrecker service? Brittmore Road?” I questioned in a low tone. “You’re in Houston? What’s going on?”

“There’s no time for all the questions, Niquole. Get on the road.”

“I don’t know where Brittmore Road is.”

“Don’t you have a GPS in your car? Use it,” he replied before hanging up.

My mind was going a million miles per minute as I wondered why he would possibly need me to meet him at a junkyard. I blushed at the thought of him wanting to try something kinky and different since we hadn’t seen each other in a while. When I finally heard Germaine walk away from the door, I quickly dried off then ran to my room and slipped on a pink velour Juicy jogging suit along with some tennis shoes.

After that was done, I raced out of the house without telling Germaine anything. When I made it outside, I realized there was no need to say goodbye because his truck was gone. I also realized that I wasn't dressed for the weather, but I didn't have time to run back inside the house and change. At just the end of June, it was hot as hell. Obviously the other summer months were going to be brutal. I hopped in my car, tapped in the directions to the wrecker service on my Navigation system and drove to my destination with the AC on full blast.

The forty-five minute drive seemed endless, but I eventually made it to the salvage yard. When I pulled into the gate, I glanced at the hours of operation and saw that the yard was closed on Sunday, so I quickly wondered how and why Kingston wanted to meet at such a strange place. However, I quickly brushed it off. I drove around and through a number of wrecked and crushed cars until I saw three Navigators parked in front of a blue, rusted garage

"What in the hell do you have up your sleeve, Kingston?" I mumbled to myself after pulling on the side of the SUVs. I grabbed my phone from the passenger seat and called him. "Baby, I'm here," I spoke when he answered. "What's going on?"

"Come in and see," he replied before hanging up.

I stepped out of my car and walked toward the doors. I then stopped in my tracks when I saw the dark skinned, burly guy from the hotel in Waco standing outside the door as if he was guarding or protecting what or who was inside. I wanted to know what was going on and why he was there. He nodded at me with a hard, stern look on his face then opened the door for me to go inside. I walked past him slowly, but never took my eyes off of him until I heard my man's voice.

"Hey," Kingston addressed me.

"Hey," I smiled curiously. "What's going on?" I asked, while glancing around the musty smelling garage. "Wasn't that the so-called bartender from Homewood Suites?" I asked looking back to find the man.

"Yeah, that's him."

"W…What is he doing here?" I stammered, thinking awful thoughts after finding out that the door had been closed behind me.

"Don't worry about him, Niquole," Kingston replied. "I've got a surprise for you. Why are you wearing that hot ass sweat suit?" he teased then eyed me up and down. "Don't you know it's gonna be in the triple digits today and probably the rest of the summer?"

"I was trying to get out of the house as fast as I could. I didn't have time to…"

"No need to explain," Kingston interrupted. "I need for you to confirm something for me."

"Confirm what?" I asked as he led me further inside the grimy garage.

"Is that him?"

"Is who who?" I reiterated.

I turned in the direction he was pointing and gasped when I saw Hummer tied to a chair. When he saw me, his eyes widened in disbelief and shock. He remembered me. I could only imagine what was going through his mind at that moment knowing that what he tried to do to me at the party was the reason he was probably tied up.

"Kingston, what in the hell are you doing?" I gasped.

"Is this the muthafucka, Niquole?"

I stared at Hummer who was trying hard to hold back his frightened tears. His hands were tied behind his back and his mouthed was covered with tape.

"Is that him?" Kingston raised his voice.

I glanced around the garage and saw a few more men

standing around waiting for Kingston's signal to demolish Hummer. Then I glanced back at Kingston and quickly wondered what I had gotten myself into.

"Niquole, is this the nigga?" he asked again. "I know it's him, but I just need you to confirm."

"H…How did you find him?" I questioned in disbelief.

"Don't worry about all of that. Is this the nigga that tried to get at you?" Kingston asked.

I glanced back up at Hummer who was pleading to me with his eyes as he struggled to free himself. If he wasn't in any pain, he surely looked uncomfortable.

"Baby, I can't let you do this," I addressed Kingston.

Kingston smiled. "I'm not gonna kill him, Niquole. Didn't you want Germaine to beat his ass?"

"Yes, but…"

"Well, I'm gonna do what he didn't do,"Kingston said as he caressed my cheeks and kissed me on the forehead. "Did you ever wonder why your bitch-ass husband didn't beat his ass?"

I was too stunned to answer him. Moments later, Kingston nodded at his boys and I knew that was the signal for them to take turns using Hummer as a punching bag. Before they could do so, I ran to Hummer and stood in front of him.

"Kingston, please don't do this!"

He waved his boys away and walked up to me. He could see the fear on my face and the scared, guilty, apologetic look on Hummer's. Kingston pulled me into his arms then whispered in my ear, "For you, I won't let them beat him," he spoke then kissed my cheek.

"Thank you," I said and blew a sigh of relief.

"Muthafucka, she just saved you from an ass whooping," he addressed Hummer.

I couldn't see Hummer's face, but I'm sure he released a sigh of relief as well. I wrapped my arms around Kingston to let him know how thankful I was. Although I was pissed at what Hummer did to me, Kingston looked as if he was there to do far more damage than what I expected.

Kingston squeezed me tighter into his chest with his left arm. It felt as if he was showing me sincerity in regards to his decision to not have Hummer mauled, but instead, he showed me something totally different and unexpected. I jumped when I suddenly heard a gunshot.

Kingston placed his left hand on the back of my head and pressed my face to his chest so that I couldn't turn around and see what he'd done. "I couldn't let that muthafucka get away with it. I protect mine, Niquole," he said then kissed me again.

I couldn't believe that he'd killed a man in my presence. My body began trembling uncontrollably as Kingston quickly walked me out of the garage. I watched as he tossed the gun in his SUV, then escort me to my car as if everything was okay. He unzipped my jacket in an attempt to remove it, but I stopped him.

"What are you doing?" I asked in panic mode.

"You have some blood on your jacket, baby. I'll get rid of it while I'm getting rid of him."

I didn't budge. I wanted him to know that I didn't want his hands on me…not now anyway. Besides, I was still in a state of shock.

"I…I…I don't have a…any…thing under here," I stuttered.

"It's cool. Just make sure you get rid of it. Damn!" Kingston cursed after noticing a few blood splatters on his burnt orange linen shirt. He removed the shirt before tucking it under his arm. "Trust me, in a few days, you'll be over this," he spoke then helped me in my car. "You didn't see any of it. As far as you're concerned, it never happened. Now, go to the studio and get yourself together before you go home. I've got some cleaning up to do. Don't look so shocked. I've shown and proved to you before that I take care of mine."

When he spoke those words, any and everything else that clouded my mind disappeared. "What did you say?" I asked, needing confirmation.

His? I questioned to myself. *What did he mean by that? Was that his way of telling me that he loved me?*

"I don't do shit like this just for anyone, Niquole. Like I told you inside, I protect mine," Kingston said then blew me a kiss with those LL Cool J lips. "Niquole, get rid of the jacket," he ordered before walking back inside the garage.

Why am I not calling the cops? I questioned myself. *Better yet, why am I not crying*? *Even worse than that, why is the shock quickly wearing off of my body?* I knew why. He and I were connected in more ways than one.

As I drove to the studio, my phone rang. I didn't want to answer it because I was still thinking about what Kingston had just done and said to me. However, whoever was calling was adamant about reaching me because the phone kept ringing. I snatched it off the passenger seat and answered the call.

"Have you lost your fucking mind? I'm happy that I just ran up the street to CVS for my damn cigarettes!" Germaine screamed into the phone nearly bursting my eardrum. "I hope whatever it is you're doing is fucking important!" he continued.

"I don't have time for this, Germaine. What are you talking about?"

"You left the damn kids in the fucking house by themselves! John John was screaming to the top his lungs when I got back!"

"Oh my God! I thought you took them with you!" I spoke frantically.

"How in the hell could you have thought that? You didn't even bother to check! I told you I was running to the store, but I guess you were too busy on the fucking phone to hear that part!"

"You always have them so I didn't think this time was

any different."

"Well, you thought wrong. Next time check before you jump to conclusions! What kind of fucking mother are you?" Germaine asked.

He hung up. Seconds later, my phone rang again. It was my mother. "What do you want?" I answered.

"Why in the hell did you leave the boys at home by themselves? What in the hell were you doing that made you forget them?"

"None of your fucking business!"

Click. I turned the phone off. That incident alone was a sure sign that I was in over my head with Kingston

"Niquole, your lunch is here," Meagan said through the speakerphone. She'd interrupted my thoughts of Kingston's actions just two days before.

"Okay. Bring it in," I replied back.

"What did you order today? It smells good," Meagan said when she stepped inside my office seconds later.

"For some reason, I've got this craving for Chinese food," I replied.

"You're not pregnant are you?"

I looked up at the blonde, wannabe black chic and frowned. "Girl, if something creeps inside of me right now, the only people who will know about it are me, the doctor and God," I laughed. She joined in on the laughter. "You can have some if you'd like. I'm sure there's more than enough," I said admiring the red, purple and black maxi dress and stiletto heels that added four inches to her five-foot-six frame. "I've got some sesame chicken, shrimp and cabbage, a few fried wontons and egg rolls," I listed, then skimmed through the bag as if I'd forgotten what I ordered.

"That sounds like a meal for four," Meagan said. "Are you expecting company?"

"If I were expecting company, do you think I would've offered you any of the food?" I joked. "Whatever I don't eat is going home to John John. He loves Chinese food. Do you want any?"

"Thanks, but no thanks," she declined. "I have a few errands to run before I get ready for the party tonight. Is it okay if I take off a few hours early?"

"As long as I don't have to take care of any messages or emails, you can take off."

"You know I've taken care of all of that," Meagan replied in a tone letting me know that she was good at her job. Hell, she was. Ever since hiring her a month after Nathan was born, she'd shown and proved to be a very valuable asset to my label.

"It's kind of quiet out there," I spoke referring to the noise that I wasn't hearing in the halls.

"Everyone's in the conference room."

"For what?"

"They wanted to hear Fortunes sing a few tunes."

"Tell those girls they better not fuck their voices up before the album release party tonight," I joked.

"I know, right? So, are you ready for that?"

"As ready as I'll ever be. Fortunes is gonna make men fall to their knees and beg to eat pussy."

Meagan smiled. "You're off the chain, Niquole, but I think you're right. The producers wrote some great tracks for them."

"I know. I got teary-eyed on a couple of them."

"Yeah, right," she laughed. "I don't think you can produce tears."

"You've got a point," I replied thinking about the tears that I tried to make fall after Kingston murdered Hummer. "Meagan, before you go, I need to talk to you about something," I added when I saw her do a ballerina twirl and start toward the door.

"What's up?"

"Close the door."

She did as advised. "What's going on?" Meagan asked

curiously after tossing her straight, blond hair over her shoulders.

I reached inside my desk drawer and pulled out a brand new black Louis Vuitton L'Absolu, leather bag with the tag still attached. I placed it on top of my desk and pushed it toward her.

"This is for you. I had it delivered today."

"Are you serious? This is what the FedEx guy dropped off today?"

"Yeah."

Meagan shook her head. "What is this for? I don't understand."

"I can't tell you now, but you'll know what it's for when and if something happens."

I had a funny feeling down in the pit of my stomach that Kingston would be making unexpected visits to the studio after what happened and I needed to make sure I had all of my ducks in a row.

Meagan gently clutched the bag then stared at me after looking at the price. "You paid thirty-five hundred bucks for this bag?" she asked shockingly. "Are you in some kind of trouble or something?"

"No. No, it's nothing like that." I smiled halfheartedly then tried to hide the worried look on my face.

"I can't accept this. This is too much," Meagan said as she pushed the bag back to me. "It feels like a bribe to keep me quiet about something. If you're in trouble, you don't have to bribe me. You're my friend. I'll do anything for you."

"Thanks, Meagan." I smiled. "Just take the bag anyway. I know how much you love purses."

"That's true, but you've got to tell me what's going on." She took a seat in one of the burgundy and pewter, barrel shaped chairs in front of my desk. She then crossed her legs as if to say, she wasn't going anywhere until I told her something.

"Meagan, it's none of your business. I just need to

know if you have my back if some shit pops off."

"Okay, Niquole, you're really starting to scare me," she replied. "Does it have anything to do with the label? Germaine? The boys? Your health?"

"Look," I huffed letting her know that she was irritating me, "I don't need this right now. I've got enough shit on my mind and I don't need you drilling me about any of it."

When Meagan saw my reaction and heard the tension in my voice, she knew not to ask anymore questions.

"Okay. I'll see you later," Meagan said before standing up. She clutched her new bag then left.

In the few months that I'd known her, Meagan had never given or caused me any trouble, so I knew that she would have my back.

I opened the brown, paper bag and soaked in the aroma of the sesame chicken and shrimp. I was famished, and couldn't open the bag fast enough. When that task was finally done, I ripped open the soy sauce and poured it all over the food then dove into it. While eating and staring around my pewter glazed office, Kingston's actions crept back into my mind. I wondered if it bothered him that I hadn't freaked out as any other normal woman would've done after practically witnessing a murder. What if our little secret would bring us even closer together? I was so wrapped in my thoughts that I didn't hear or see Germaine walk inside the office moments later.

"We need to talk," he spoke sternly after sitting down in front of me.

"Couldn't this wait until I got home? I'm trying to have lunch," I pouted.

"If it could've, I wouldn't be here right now."

I pushed my food away and leaned back in my high-back, leather executive chair. I then folded my arms across my chest and waited for what he had to say. Before he could begin, Meagan reentered my office. Germaine flinched a little when he heard her voice, but I didn't think anything of it.

“I’m sorry to interrupt,” she spoke from the door. “FedEx just delivered another package and they need to check your ID,” she addressed me.

“Check my ID?” I questioned. “I’ve never heard of shit like that before.”

Meagan shrugged her shoulders. “He said the sender requested it.”

I opened my desk drawer and retrieved my ID from my purse then stood up and walked to the lobby with Meagan by my side.

“What do you think it is?” she asked curiously.

“I don’t know, but it better be something good to cause all of this hoopla.”

“Seems like the FedEx guy came at a perfect time.”

“What do you mean?”

“I could feel the tension in your office between you and Germaine.”

“Meagan, leave it alone,” I said before stopping in front of the cute, tanned, delivery man who gave me the most electrifying smile.

“Are you Niquole Wright?” he asked.

I presented my ID to him. After signing my name on their little electronic device, he handed me a huge, purple and black striped box. I thought it was going to be heavy because of its size but, it wasn’t. It couldn’t have weighed more than two pounds.

“He was cute,” Meagan spoke after the delivery guy walked away.

“He hasn’t left yet. Go talk to him,” I giggled as I watched her get all googly-eyed over the guy.

“He doesn’t make enough money for me,” she joked.

We both laughed.

“I wonder what in the hell could be in here?” I questioned before slightly shaking the box.

“Did you order something and forgot about it?” she

asked.

"Possibly, but there's only one way to find out."

When we walked back to my office, Germaine was still sitting with an uneasy look on his face.

"What's in the box?" he asked.

"Your guess is as good as mine," I replied.

"I'll bet it's something else that you don't need, don't use or have any room for," he replied in a slightly nasty tone.

I rolled my eyes at him and placed the box on my desk accidentally knocking down my favorite photo of Johnathan and Nathan asleep. They were both passed out on their backs in the same snow angel position. Curiously, I lifted the top off the box and retrieved the card that was lying on top of some white tissue paper. I slapped Meagan's hand away when I saw her trying to lift and peak underneath. I pulled the card from the envelope and held back my ecstatic emotion when I read it.

This should help take your mind off of things.
I want this on your body tonight at the party.
Love,
Kingston

I eased the card back into the envelope and slid it in the front pocket of my Nicole Miller slacks. I tried to hold back my excitement as I dove through the tissue paper. When I finally saw what was inside, I gasped…so did Meagan. Germaine wanted to see what the excitement was all about so he stood up and glanced inside the box as well.

"Girl, how could you forget that you ordered this?" Meagan spoke enthusiastically as she lifted the dress from the box and pranced around the office with it. "Isn't this nice, Germaine?" she addressed him.

"Yeah," he answered quickly then sat back down.

I could never understand why he was always acting uneasy around her. I knew they weren't fucking. I just brushed it off as another black man afraid to be around white people. I could feel Germaine's eyes on me as he waited for me to answer Meagan's question.

"I've been so damn swamped with the last minute details for the album release party that I forgot it was being delivered today," I lied.

"Please tell me that you're wearing this to the party?" Meagan continued. "If not, can I borrow it?" she joked.

"I gotta be fly, don't I?" I laughed, hoping Germaine couldn't figure out that I was making everything up as I went along. "Meagan, put the dress back in the box before it gets dirty."

"Yeah, I'd better because I can't afford to replace it. Prada is definitely not in my budget," she giggled. "I need to head out anyway," she said after placing the dress back inside the box. "I'll see y'all later," she added before bouncing out the door.

"What did you want to talk to me about?" I asked Germaine then placed the top back over the box.

I really didn't care what was on his mind. I just didn't need him questioning me about the dress. I rubbed my hand over the box as if it meant the world to me. I was so wrapped up in my new gift that I wasn't paying any attention to the fact that he was watching my every move. He knew there was more to the dress than I was letting on.

"So, you have a separate bank account that you're hiding from me?" he asked with piercing eyes. I knew what he was talking about, but couldn't figure out how he knew about it.

I glanced down at my computer. "Why are you snooping through my shit, Germaine?"

"It was in plain sight. I didn't have to snoop, but don't try to avoid the subject. What's the account for? Why didn't I know about it?"

I held back the bull that was raging inside of me, but I knew it would be even more suspicious if I prolonged an answer. "The account is for the boys."

"The boys?" he asked rhetorically.

"Yes. College and shit like that. Don't you want the best for your kids?"

"Of course. But why did you feel the need to hide that from me?"

"I don't have to tell you everything that I do with my money."

"Well, if it's for the boys then I'll need the code," he stated.

"For what?"

"Because their my kids too, and I should always know what's going on."

I had to laugh. "Germaine, I hope that's not why you're here. If so, you're wasting your damn time. I'm not giving you anything to…"

"You know what," he interrupted before tossing a plastic Target bag at me. "I don't want to hear that same ole BS. Explain that!" He pointed at the bag.

"What's this?" I asked, slowly opening the bag.

"You tell me."

Once the bag was opened, I held back the shock that I wanted to show on my face and the gasp that wanted to escape my mouth. *Fuck. Why didn't I get rid of that shit*? I thought after glancing at the pink, blood-splattered jacket.

"Where did you get this?"

"I was in your car early this morning looking for one of Nathan's diaper bags. I couldn't confront you about it then because you dashed out right after I walked back inside the house. Now, answer my question, what is it?"

"I don't appreciate you going through my shit, Germaine."

"It's your jacket. You should know what the hell is on it." His voice grew curious. "Is that blood, Nikki?" he asked before snatching the bag out of my hand.

I quickly snatched it back and frowned. "You need to

mind your own damn business," I said after turning away from him with the Target bag clutched tightly in my hands. I couldn't face him. I couldn't think of a lie fast enough and damn sure wasn't about to tell him the truth. At that moment, I wish I had let Kingston take the jacket with him and drove to the studio like he instructed.

"Look, I don't have time for this shit, Germaine. I've got a party to get ready for. Now, will you please leave?" I finally turned to face him.

He stared at me with a blank look on his face as if nothing that I said or did could stun or shock him anymore.

"What?" I barked.

He shook his head before asking, "Since you can't explain the jacket then can you explain this receipt I found in the trunk as well?"

I snatched the receipt he pulled from his pocket. I then swallowed the lump in my throat as I stared down at the paper. It was for a four thousand dollar pair of diamond, baguette studs and a two thousand dollar TAG Heuer men's watch.

"I know you're not buying *those* kinds of gifts for potential clients are you? And I know they're not for me because you haven't bought me anything in a while."

Germaine stood there like a detective waiting for a confession. It pained me when I made my next move. I opened my bottom desk drawer and pulled out a blue and black striped wrapped box.

"I wanted to surprise you."

"You're kidding me, right?" he laughed after pushing the box that I tried to hand him.

"Fine! Be ungrateful!" I snapped and dropped the box back into the drawer, happy that I didn't have to give Kingston's gifts away.

"Nikki, where in the hell am I gonna put the earrings? My ears aren't fucking pierced," Germaine seethed then pointed to his earlobes. "And you know I could care less about expensive watches. I can tell time just fine on this ten-year-old Citizens," he said tapping the worn watch.

I needed to get him out of my shit, but didn't know how. To my surprise, he did it for me.

"Don't hurt yourself thinking of a lie, Nikki. Just remember this. What's done in the dark always comes to the light," Germaine said before gliding toward the door. He bumped into Jalisa on his way out.

Shit! I didn't feel like being bothered by her either. She was wearing a pair of Jimmy Choo Verity sandals and a black spaghetti strap mini dress. Her long, black hair was pulled back into a very stylish ponytail. She was always in model mode.

"Hi, Germaine," she greeted him with a smile.

"What's up, Jalisa?" he replied nonchalantly.

Jalisa glanced at me and gave me a look of wonderment. I guess she figured by Germaine's reply that I'd said something to put him in such a mood.

"Well, can I at least get a hug?" she addressed him. "I haven't seen you in a while."

They embraced for a few seconds while I picked through my food that I no longer desired due to the unwanted interruptions. After the hug, he tried to walk out, but Jalisa grabbed his hand. "Are you okay?"

"Ask your damn friend," Germaine nodded toward me then walked out.

Jalisa walked toward the chairs in front of my desk as if she was walking down a runway. She then sat down and crossed one long leg over the other. But when she opened her mouth to speak, I stopped her.

"Before you ask me anything about Germaine, save it."

"Actually, I was going to ask why you've been avoiding my calls."

"Jalisa, you know I'm busy."

"With work or *him*?

I glared at her and answered, "Both. Conversations about him are off limits as well," I warned. She knew I meant business.

"How are the boys?"

"They're fine. How are you and that guy Austin doing?" I quickly changed the subject.

"His ass is out the door. I had to get a restraining order against him because that fool went psycho on me when we were in Paris."

"What?"

"Yeah. He was jealous of my blossoming success and tried to start using me as a punching bag." My eyes widened as she continued. "He hit me once and that was all it took. I kicked him out of my loft and he would show up at my modeling gigs causing a mess. I had to move because he kicked my door in."

"Damn, Jalisa, are you alright?"

"As long as I carry my nine by my side, I'm good. Now, I know why my dad got me those lessons at the gun range," she laughed.

I returned the laughter because I remembered those days at the gun range. She was fierce with a gun and anyone would be a fool to be staring down the barrel of it. "So, how long are you here for?" I asked.

"For a few months. You know there's no place like home."

"If you want to get technical about it, your home is in New Orleans," I reminded.

"You know what I mean. I foolishly followed family," she replied. "The contractor is ready to start the renovations on my condo."

"So, are you staying with your folks until it's done?"

"Are you crazy? I love my family, but I hate them as well. I'm staying in one of the model condos until it's done."

"Cool." I was hoping I'd given her enough friendly

chit chat because I was ready for her to leave.

"So, you went to see Kingston the other day when you hung up on me, huh?"

"I knew it was coming," I mumbled.

"I'm assuming you did by your reactions. I've got to ask you this, Nikki. Why did you even marry Germaine?"

I cut my eyes at her. "I've told you before and I'll tell you again. I thought he loved me until he deceived me just like all the others."

"The man wanted to have a kid, Nikki. What was wrong with that?"

"This conversation is over." I wasn't about to sit and listen to that crap.

"Why don't you just leave if you don't love him anymore?" Jalisa questioned.

Between her and my mother, I don't know who got on my nerves the most.

"Bitch, what do you think I'm trying to do?" Her eyes widened in disbelief. "It's time for you to leave," I spoke sternly after standing up and walking toward the door to let her know that I was serious.

"Wow! You're kicking me out?"

"I told you that Kingston was off limits and now, you're bringing up this bullshit about Germaine so, yes you have to go. I have shit to do anyway."

"Okay…okay. I won't bring them up anymore," Jalisa tried to convince.

"Yes, you will and you know it so to keep me from cursing you out when you do, I think it's best that you leave."

"Listen, I came by to see if we could have lunch and do some catching up," Jalisa continued as if she was prolonging her departure.

"As you can see on my desk, I have lunch," I replied. "Look, I'll just see you at the party."

She stood up with much attitude and walked out without a goodbye. I didn't care that she was pissed. I was tired of her being in my business. After closing and locking the door, I walked back over to my desk then dropped in my chair and blew a long sigh of relief. Germaine was getting too close for comfort and I needed to get my act together before he got any closer. Logging onto my online bank account, I skimmed over my get-a-way account and smiled. Me, Kingston and the boys were gonna be set once I left Germaine.

My smile turned to a frown when I opened my email account and saw a message from my blackmailer. I slapped my hands across my mouth to keep from screaming when I opened up a few pictures of me and Kingston going in and out of different hotels. I knew I had to put the Niquole and Kingston plan into full force action before that son-of-a-bitch exposed me to the world. In the meantime, I prepared to visit my bank for the new wire transfer.

I was eager and anxious to get inside of The Roxy for Fortunes' album release party partly because I knew this female group was gonna blow up, but mainly because I was dying to see Kingston. I was apprehensive about inviting him, but couldn't deny him access into my world after receiving his breathtaking, unexpected gift.

When the limo pulled up to The Roxy's entrance, a slew of reporters and photographers were waiting for my arrival. It didn't take long for the handsome, freckle faced limo driver to open my door and extend his hand to me which also came along with a wide face smile. It seemed like he'd been practicing before picking me up. As soon as he helped me out, the camera flashes started as well as the chatter. I glanced on both sides of the red carpet and noticed that the reporters and photographers were held at bay by purple, velvet ropes that were the same shade as my dress. It was my time to shine.

I placed my right foot on the carpet to show off my stunning, five-inch, Prada stilettos. When the flashes died down, I gracefully struck a pose with a huge, bright smile on my face. I was the shit and I knew it. I floated down the red carpet in the beautiful dress that I felt obligated to flaunt knowing that *he* was going to be at the party. I continued to smile at all of the cameras as I made my way inside the club forgetting the fact that I had left Germaine behind. There was no need to flaunt him by my side when he wasn't the one that I wanted to be there with anyway. Besides, we hadn't spoken to each other since he walked out of my office earlier that day.

I was excited to see the place packed from wall to wall with fans, rival label mates and top executives. I knew there was gonna be a huge turnout, but this was beyond what I expected. It made me realize that I was on my way up. I made a mental note to purchase Meagan another bag because she'd outdone herself as usual. The pink and purple strobe lights did it for me because she knew those were my favorite colors. It didn't take long for me to make my rounds and mingle while secretly searching for Kingston. Germaine had become close friends with many of my associates and clients, so I knew he wouldn't be bothering me for much of the night.

I walked and smiled at the spectators and accepted numerous praises and congratulations. I paused when one of them decided to grab my arm. My heart skipped a few beats because I knew it was Kingston. I frowned when I turned around and saw that it wasn't.

"Nice party, Niquole."

I stared at one of my rivals and fought back the urge to roll my eyes and walk off.

"Thanks, A.J." I forced a smile then stared into his gray, hypnotic eyes. I glanced around the room so that I wouldn't fall under his spell as I had once before. "What are you doing here anyway? Shouldn't you be back in Louisiana tending to your own label?"

"Damn, is that how you greet me?" he asked cynically. A.J. and I had history; history that continued into the present. "I came by to show my support. I can't wait to hear these new girls that you've signed."

Why was he lying? I knew he could care less. "If I were a naïve bitch, I'd believe you."

"I'm not lying, baby. I wish you much success since most of it belongs to me," he smiled, then attempted to kiss my cheek. I pulled back for fear that Kingston would see. "What's wrong? It would be just like old times. You said it best; what no one knows won't hurt them."

"Bye, A.J.," I tried to stomp away, but he stopped me.

"You don't want our little secret to come out, do you?" he asked.

"You don't want our little secret to come out either. Do you think your wife will stay married to you if it does? And when she does leave you, she's taking more than half," I replied with a fierce look on my face. "I'm done with you, A.J. You had your chance."

"Now, you're lying. Even after our bullshit, you still couldn't and can't resist me. 'Til this day, I still think your oldest son is mine," he replied with a huge grin.

"I assure you that he's not and if he was, would you take care of him?" I asked cynically already knowing the answer would be no.

"I take care of mine, Niquole."

"Yeah. When you have no other choice."

"How 'bout I fly you out to New Orleans like old times?" A.J. asked as he slowly grinded up against me."

I needed him to stop. He was taking me back to the days and nights he would send my body into an orgasmic fury. I quickly obliterated those images and climbed down off that cloud when I thought about Kingston.

"No," I answered bluntly. "You need to move before you get me in trouble," I scolded and gently shoved him off of me.

"With who? Germaine?" he laughed. "That nigga has his nose wide open for you."

"For your information, I'm not talking about Germaine," I said and rolled my neck.

"Enlighten me."

"What is it that Jay-Z says? I'm on to the next one."

"So, you're still fooling around on your husband,

huh?"

He didn't need to know all my business. "No, I only fooled around on him with you even after our piece of shit relationship went sour."

"Liar. Why did you even marry him?"

"Why did you marry your wife?" I returned.

"You should've just stayed single if you're gonna be available to men like that."

"So, you're calling me a whore now?" I chuckled.

"If the shoe fits, wear it…and it looks to me like you're wearing it well," he said after glancing down at my shoes. "I've had you a few times since you've been married and I'm more than sure this new nigga has, too. Ain't no telling how many have been in between."

"The world will never know," I winked.

I hated it when his Lamman Rucker looking-ass smiled at me with those mesmerizing, eyes and smooth brown skin. I was a sucker for them both. I hadn't been with A.J. in over a year. In fact, I never should've fucked around with him after we left each other alone. We both had done dirt to each other, but one thing was for certain, he was a great fuck if not the greatest I'd ever had.

"I'll be in town for a few more days. Get at me. I'm sure you still have the number," he said before stealing a kiss then walking away.

A.J. was a bold one and that was why I couldn't leave him alone. We were the black version of the War of the Roses couple; minus the marriage. I regrouped once I realized I was in the packed club with thousands of eyes and four of them belonged to Germaine and Kingston.

For about an hour, I engaged in several conversations while secretly scouring the room for my man. I then grew uneasy when I couldn't find him. Trying to contain my anger, I downed glasses of champagne when the waiter or waitresses walked past me with their trays filled with neatly organized champagne flutes. When I felt my phone vibrate in my purse, the flute that I was holding instantly hit the floor. The group that I was supposedly conversing with stared at me with curious eyes. I guess they were trying to see if I was drunk, but I wasn't. I just wanted that vibration in my purse to be from Kingston.

"Excuse me," I said to them before departing.

As I gently pushed through the crowd, I rummaged through my purse for my phone. I located it as soon as I stopped in front of the bathroom. I blew a sigh of relief when I saw *Mercy* flash across the fuchsia, backlit screen.

"Hello?" I answered after covering my left ear so that I could hear.

"You look so beautiful."

"Where are you?" I asked while scoping the room with a huge smile on my face.

"I'm here watching you."

"I want to see you."

All of a sudden, I caught a pair of eyes staring at me from across the room.

"Do you see me now?" Kingston asked as he flashed those bright whites that complimented his dark skin so well. If I hadn't known who he was, I would've mistaken him for Tyrese Gibson. "There's a door leading upstairs to your right. Meet me there," he said before hanging up.

I watched him glide across the room in his white, button down shirt and blue jeans. His demeanor made the simple outfit look like platinum. I watched as several females cut their eyes at him as he walked past. They obviously wanted what I was about to go get, but they could cancel that shit. I wasn't about to share my man.

When I located Germaine in the crowd and saw that he was still busy chatting and getting hammered, I decided to make my move. The crowd was thick which made my journey extremely hard, especially with everyone stopping to congratulate me. I didn't wanna be rude, so I stopped to chit-chat for as long as I could, but eventually had to excuse myself. Besides, I wasn't paying attention to any of that shit anyway. My focus was on that door, and after shaking several more hands, I finally made it. I turned to see if anyone was watching me before I disappeared on the other side.

"What took you so long?" Kingston asked.

"My party," I answered, then quickly changed the subject. "Kingston, we have a problem."

"I'm sure it's nothing that I can't handle. What is it?"

"Germaine found the jacket."

"What jacket?"

"The one with Hummer's blood on it."

His eyes increased. "Damn it, Niquole! What the fuck?"

I jumped at his harsh tone, but could understand his anger.

"Where's the jacket now?"

"I threw it away," I lied.

"Next time when I tell you to let me handle something, let me handle it, okay?" he said in a sexy yet soft, aggressive tone.

"Okay," I agreed.

"Now, back to you. Why did you cut and dye your hair?" Kingston asked as he ran his fingers through my new, jet black layered bob.

"I didn't think you'd notice," I blushed.

"I notice everything about you," he winked.

Before I could speak another word, he pushed me against the wall.

I smiled seductively. "I see that you miss me, too."

He lifted me off the floor and attacked my neck with those juicy lips. My chest soon received the same attention. I slapped my hands against the concrete wall and clawed at it with my French manicured nails. Closing my eyes, I was slowly slipping into ecstasy; a place where I easily slipped into whenever I was with him.

"Kingston, we can't do this here," I breathed in his ear when his fingers slipped under my dress.

"You just don't know how bad I want you right now," he replied. "You look so damn good in the dress. I knew you would."

I grabbed his cheeks and pulled his lips to mine. I needed to taste them. However, we both jumped when the door swung open and two men and a woman appeared. They seemed to be drunk as they giggled, slurred and staggered.

"Sorry," one of the men apologized as he led the others back into the party then closed the door.

"Kingston, we need to get back," I spoke frantically. "We're gonna get caught."

He ignored me as well as the close call. Moments later, he slowly lifted my dress then pushed my body against the door so that no one could open it again. My heart rate instantly began to increase as he slipped my thongs to the side and fingered me until I was drenching wet. It never took long for me to get in the zone. I listened to my pussy smack her lips as he fingered me faster and faster.

Kingston could feel me squirming "You think she's ready, baby?"

"Yes," I whimpered.

He unzipped his pants then glided his love stick inside of me.

"Kingston…Kingston," I moaned softly. I wrapped my arms around his neck and my legs around his waist.

"I hear you, baby. Talk to me."

I licked my full lips. "Oh God!"

"Baby, he ain't nowhere up in here. It's all Kingston."

I moaned and breathed heavily as I took all of him. Even though there's no such thing as a quickie with Kingston, I had to rush both our orgasms before people started looking for me. I groped his soft, pimple free ass, pushed him deeper inside of me then started my thrust workout on him. I wanted us both to climax together. Seconds later, I got my wish as we both erupted. I covered his mouth because I knew when Kingston reached his peak, he was known to get loud. With the music on full blast, I'm sure no one would've have heard him, but I didn't wanna take any chances.

After catching our breaths, he set me down. Luckily for me, I was carrying my purse. I never left home without feminine wipes or body spray, so I pulled out one of my wipes and ripped it open.

"You're gonna do that now?" Kingston asked as I wiped all the cum from between my legs.

"Duh. I can't do it out there," I giggled.

He didn't bother to respond. Instead, he rushed back inside the club leaving me behind to clean up our mess. *Damn you could've at least given me a kiss*, I thought to myself after pulling my dress back down. Five minutes later, I reentered the club and stopped dead in my tracks when I ran into Germaine.

"What were you doing?" he glanced over me like I was hiding something.

"I…I needed some air," I stuttered hoping that he didn't see Kingston walk out of the door before me.

"You needed some air, huh?"

"Yes, I needed some damn air," I replied harshly then tried to walk off. He grabbed my arm and jerked me back toward him. "Germaine, let go of me," I ordered.

"Tell me what were you doing, Nikki?"

I glanced around the room and noticed a number of eyes on us. He was not about to punk me at my own damn party. I jerked from his grasp. "Don't you ever put your damn hands on me like that again! What the hell is wrong with you? I told you I needed some air!" I tried to walk away, but Germaine snatched me again. This time, it was a little harder and caused me to stumble.

"Don't walk away from me like that. I'm trying to talk to you."

I could smell the alcohol on his breath. I couldn't believe that he was nearly drunk already. As I was about to light into him, I managed to spot Kingston at the bar tossing back tequila shots. He was too occupied in a conversation to witness what was going on with me. Part of me wanted him to come to my rescue, but I knew that wouldn't be wise. I frowned as I watched a woman peck Kingston's cheek then slide her fingers between his. She seemed a little bit too comfortable for her to be one of the hoochies in the club then I saw it; her ring finger. She was his wife.

Chapter Nine

Why in the hell did he bring her here? The invitation had been extended to him and him only. Not that tall, beautiful, curvaceous, caramel-skinned knockout that was falling all over him. Her big, bright smile even made me melt so I knew what it did for him. I wanted to dash toward her, snatch her by her weave, then throw her ass out. I hated watching her fall all over him and rub on his arm like that was her fucking job. As hard as it was to admit…I knew by my reaction that I was jealous. But I had to get control of my emotions because there was another matter at hand that I needed to take care of.

"Germaine, I'm not doing this here with you tonight. Let me go before I have security handle your ass," I threatened.

"You're gonna get security to handle me?" he laughed. "You're a piece of work, Nikki. A piece of fucking work."

Before I had the chance to retaliate, Jalisa jumped between us. "This is neither the time nor the place for this," she addressed us both with worry painted all over her face. "Don't do this here. This is not what you want to see in the papers, blogs or websites."

Jalisa was right. I didn't need that kind or negative publicity. Germaine knew that I was serious so he released me and walked off to escape anymore embarrassment.

"What's your damn problem, Nikki?" Jalisa scolded

me.

"Bitch, he was the one who grabbed me!"

"Did he have reason to?"

I jerked my head back at her question. "Did he have reason to?" I asked rhetorically.

"I saw you go in and out that door with a guy. I assume he's Kingston."

"Why in the fuck are you watching me like a damn stalker? You're the damn model. Folks should be watching *you,* not the other way around!"

Jalisa stared me up and down. "Did you just fuck him?" she asked appalled. I assumed she drew her own conclusions when I didn't answer. "That's fucking nasty," she added.

"No nastier than what you and I did in high school," I retaliated.

I struck a nerve.

"You need to watch yourself. You're wrong for bringing that up. Dead wrong," Jalisa said.

"Bitch, fuck you or better yet, go find you a man to take care of that for you," I flipped, then pushed her out of my way.

My emotions soon took their toll on me when I glanced back in Kingston's direction again. Trying to hold back the tears, I walked to the far end of the club, pulled out my phone and quickly sent him a text. I watched as he read the message from his Blackberry then whisper something in his wife's ear before walking away. Moments later, he was standing in front of me.

"Why did you bring her here?" I barked when he reached me. At that point, I didn't care if Germaine was watching me or not. I needed answers.

"Hold on, sweetie. Who do you think you're talking to like that?" he replied in a manly tone.

I quickly changed my tone. "Kingston, why did you bring her here? She doesn't need to be here."

"She's with me tonight. That's why she's here," he answered like he didn't owe me an explanation.

When he spoke those words, my heart sank. *How could he fuck me and go right back to her like nothing happened between us*? Yes, I was literally in over my head. I didn't bother to respond. My heart had split in two and confusion began to consume my brain. I gave him one last painful glare and stomped away.

"Are you okay?" Meagan asked when she saw me leaning against the bar. "Who are you staring at?"

"No one," I responded not wanting her in my business. Besides, how could I explain that I was staring at the wife of my lover? "I'm okay, Meagan," I lied.

"Fortunes is about to go on stage."

"Okay," I said before downing a glass of champagne.

I gestured for the waiter to refill my glass which he did. I could tell by the worried look on Meagan's face that she knew something was bothering me, but couldn't figure it out. I emptied the second champagne glass in less than ten seconds.

"What's up, Niquole?" Meagan whispered in my ear. "Talk to me," she said with a hint of concern in her voice.

"Leave it alone, Meagan."

She turned in the direction I was staring. "I'm going up to VIP. Are you coming?"

"I'll be up there in a minute," I lied.

She gave me one last worried look before walking off. Minutes later, the four-girl group, Fortunes, took the stage. I eased through the thick crowd on the floor instead of going to the VIP section that had been set up for me. I no longer felt important and it was all because of Kingston allowing his wife to tag along to my party. Seconds later, the strobe lights clicked off, the house lights dimmed, then the music began. I listened to the soft ballad and allowed a tear to slip from my eye when they sung the hook.

I need you to walk away from me. My heart and soul won't let me do... the thing I know I need to do...and that's let you go. I need you to walk away from me.

The words dug deep in my heart. I quickly hated and regretted the fact that we picked that song as the first single. I didn't want to hear that shit right now. It didn't take long for me to locate Kingston and his wife again. She was standing in front of him and he had his arms wrapped around her. They even had the nerve to be rocking from side to side. It was in that brief moment when I knew why my emotions were running wild. I was deeply in love with Kingston. My eyes stayed fixated on him throughout the song and although he was wrapped up with his wife, I knew that he was eyeing me from his dark, stunna shades. *Why else would he have them on?* I felt him staring at me at least I hoped he was.

When the song ended, I made a mad dash to the bathroom where I shed a few tears while staring at myself in the mirror. "Why the fuck is that bitch with my man?" I asked my reflection. "She can't have him! She can't have him! He's supposed to be with me!"

I caught a glimpse of two women staring at me and whispering. I'm sure they thought my ass was crazy.

"What in the hell are you looking at?" I lashed out at them. I was ready for a battle if they wanted one.

To my surprise, instead of responding they just laughed and walked out.

Trying to wipe the mascara that had run down my cheeks, I yanked a paper towel from the dispenser on the wall, and dabbed my face. I took a few deep breaths before freshening up my makeup and reentering the party. My eyes went straight toward the bar where Kingston and his wife were now standing. He caught a glimpse of me eyeing them like a hawk. Taunting me even more, he winked at me then kissed her red painted lips. I still couldn't understand how he could be so heartless when I knew he cared for me. He had to pay for his actions. I needed to make him feel like he'd made a huge mistake.

As much as I didn't want to, I scoured the room for Germaine. I needed to use him to my advantage. When I spotted him, I walked toward his ass like a woman on a mission. Luckily, Kingston was still staring at me. When I reached Germaine, I grabbed him and pulled his face to mine. I could tell that he was a little shocked by my actions from his resistance, but eventually gave in to the kiss. Pouring more gasoline onto the fire, I wrapped my arms around his neck and pulled him closer. I cringed when I felt his dick rise. I couldn't take it anymore.

Even though I'd pulled away, I could tell Germaine was still stunned because his dick had yet to go down. However, when I glanced over his shoulder, Kingston was no longer at the bar. I anxiously scanned the room. Neither he nor his wife was anywhere to be found. I assumed my show had pissed Kingston off and made him jealous enough to leave.

Can't take seeing your woman with another man, huh Kingston? I thought to myself just before Germaine came up and gave me a wet sloppy kiss.

"What's the problem?" he asked when I gave him the look of death. After my so called display of affection, I knew he was confused.

I guess it didn't help when I swept the back of my hand across my lips. "You need a fucking Altoid," I said before walking off.

Chapter Ten

"Germaine, where'd you put Nathan's diaper rash cream?" I yelled outside when I walked to the back door.

"It should be in his crib!" he yelled back.

"Why would you leave it there?" I frowned before stomping away.

Before I could make it upstairs to change Nathan's diaper, my cell phone rang. I pulled it from the back pocket of my True Religion jeans and frowned again once I saw Jalisa's name. I knew that if I didn't answer, she would hang up and call right back, so I quickly prepared myself for the conversation that I didn't want to have.

"Yeah?" I answered irritated. I wasn't in the mood to talk on the phone, let alone to her. She'd been more of a burden lately than a friend.

"Well, damn, that's a nice greeting."

"What do you want, Jalisa?" I asked as I entered the boys' room. I quickly placed Nathan on the changing table. But instead of taking off his diaper, I paced the floor instead.

"Let's hang out."

"Hang out?"

"Yeah. A movie? Lunch? Shopping?"

"Naw. I'm spending time with the boys today."

"Well, can I drop by and see them? I'm sure they've grown an inch since I last saw them."

I shook my head. "Not a good idea. Maybe some other time."

There was a brief pause. I counted down the seconds for her to bring up the album release party.

"So, are we just gonna dance around this or what?"

"I was waiting for you to make the first move," I sassed.

"You know that shit was foul, Nikki. Germaine doesn't deserve what you do to him."

"Fuck, Germaine. I don't deserve to be unhappy which I am with him."

"If you're so unhappy then why don't you just leave him?"

"Trust me, it's in the works. Me and my man are gonna be together real soon."

The phone went silent for a minute. I knew what she was thinking about and I was more than sure that she'd be reminding me of it shortly.

"This is high school shit all over again."

"Here we go," I said.

"You got Mr. Hughes fired from his job because of your affair. He didn't deserve that."

"No, let me correct you. He got himself fired. He shouldn't have fed me all those damn lies about us being together and shit when I graduated."

"Nikki, you threw yourself at that man."

"He didn't have to take the fucking bait. All he had to do was leave his wife and he'd still have his fucking job."

"Are you serious?" Jalisa laughed in disbelief.

It was time for me to set her ass straight because I think she must've forgotten her role in the Mr. Hughes incident. "Jalisa, weren't you in the room with the two of us one night? You don't remember the two of us seducing him?" I reminded.

"I did that shit for you!" she screamed into the phone

causing me to push it away from my ear.

"But, you did it," I laughed knowing that bitch remembered. She just wanted to forget. I remembered like it was yesterday.

Mr. Hughes and I had rented a room and I invited Jalisa. Neither of them knew about my plan. Jalisa thought it was another high school party and Mr. Hughes thought it was just another one of our rendezvous. Mr. Hughes had just stepped out of the shower when Jalisa knocked on the door. He gave me a scared look, but I assured him that everything was okay and that I had a surprise for him. I opened the door.

"Niquole, what's going on?" he asked with a curious, yet concerned look on his face when he saw Jalisa.

"Can she join?" I asked when Jalisa stepped inside.

"Whoa," Jalisa exclaimed. "What's going on? I thought this was a party."

"It is. Just the three of us. I need you to help me get my man," I whispered in her ear.

"This is crazy. I can't do this. I won't do this," Jalisa panicked.

"Yes, you can. You're my friend. Help me get my man," I pleaded.

I glanced back at Mr. Hughes who was still sporting a curious look on his face. I had to get things going. At that moment, I pulled Jalisa's face to mine and kissed her. She tried to resist, but I kept a firm grip on her face.

"Nikki are you fucking crazy?" she blasted at me when I released her face.

Mr. Hughes couldn't believe what was going on. If only he knew the lengths I'd go through to make him want me and only me.

"Jalisa, please," I begged. "I will never ask you to do anything else like this. You know you want to. Look how fine he is." I pointed to my man.

"Are you sure about this, Nikki?" Jalisa's voice trem-

bled.

"I'm more than sure," I replied as I leaned in and kissed her pink, glossed lips again. This time, there was no resistance.

I slid my fingers between hers and led her over to Mr. Hughes whose eyes agreed to allow Jalisa in our mix. I knew that I'd have questions to answer later on, but until then, we were going to have some fun. I stood in front of Mr. Hughes while Jalisa stood behind him.

"Now, do you see how much I really love you?" I addressed him. "The feeling should be mutual and I'm gonna make sure that it is."

I traced my wet tongue across his lips then forced it inside his mouth. After a few seconds of kissing, I pulled Jalisa from behind him and pressed them against each other. After a few seconds of uncomfortable eye contact between the two, their lips met. Mine soon joined in. The kiss turned into a three-way. Once we got the rhythm, we went back and forth to one another. He watched her remove my clothes and then watched me remove hers. We both removed his. Eventually, our clothes were scattered all over the floor.

"Are you sure about this, Nikki?" Jalisa whispered in my ear while Mr. Hughes' lips and tongue showed much attention to the nape of my neck.

"I love him, Jalisa. I'll do anything to get him."

She slowly pulled my face to hers and we engaged in a long, passionate kiss. Seconds later, Mr. Hughes lifted me off of the floor and onto the desk. He positioned Jalisa on the floor between my legs. He lifted my pussy up to his face and went to town on it while he fucked Jalisa in the mouth.

"I'll never forget it, Nikki, but I've put it behind me," Jalisa said, ruining my trip down memory lane.

I snickered. "That night is something you can never forget."

"So, what's your excuse about that record exec, A.J.? I

saw him at the party. Did you?"

I could hear the arrogance in her voice. She needed to be shut down and quick. "Really? Really, Jalisa? Are we gonna go down the list of all the men I've fucked or better yet, fucked over?"

"You're so damn selfish. You always need to have your way no matter who you hurt. You're never gonna change," Jalisa spat.

"Why should I? I love being me. Is your life so fucked up that you have to keep yourself wrapped up in mine?"

"Don't flatter yourself."

"Bitch, if you're gonna always talk about my so called wrongdoings when you call me, think twice before you do."

I disconnected the call. I'd heard enough of that bull. Peeping outside, I wanted to make sure that my conversation didn't catch Germaine's attention, but it didn't. He was lying on one of the lounge chairs playing catch with Johnathan who was still in the pool.

Suddenly, the doorbell rang causing me to jump. After forgetting all about Nathan's soiled diaper, I erased me and Jalisa's conversation from my mind and went to answer the door.

"Who is it?" I asked holding Nathan in my arms.

"It's Tyrell."

I took a deep breath and sighed before opening the door. "He's out back," I informed Tyrell of Germaine's whereabouts.

"How are you today, Nikki?" Tyrell asked as if I'd insulted him by not speaking.

"I'm fine," I answered snobbishly.

"I heard that was a nice album release party," he said after walking inside.

"Thanks."

"Some of the guys that were on security detail work on the police force with me."

"Great," I answered nonchalantly hoping he'd realize

that I didn't give a damn.

"So, when is the next party?"

I glanced back at Tyrell and slightly rolled my eyes to let him know that I wasn't about to engage in small talk. I couldn't help but wonder if he was trying to get under my skin. If he was, he was fucking with the right one at the right time. Jalisa had pissed me off by opening up old wounds. Not to mention, I was still pissed off at Kingston for bringing his wife to my party.

"Not sure," was all I said.

While leading Tyrell to the back door, I couldn't help but question what woman in her right mind would want to marry such an overly buff man. His neck was so fat that he looked like he was constantly struggling to breathe. When Germaine first introduced me to him, it took everything in me not to laugh. Now, every time I looked at him, I fought back the urge to snicker because he reminded me of the comedian, Lavell Crawford.

"Hey, Ty, what's going on, man?" Germaine greeted when his friend stepped out the back door.

I was about to retreat back upstairs to finally change Nathan, but wanted to hear Germaine's response when Tyrell asked if I was on the rag or something. I hid on the side of the door and waited. Germaine just laughed it off by saying I was always on the rag. I wanted to barge outside and curse his ass out, but held my cool.

As soon as I stepped away from the door, I heard Tyrell mention Hummer's name. Stopping in my tracks, I quickly turned back around so I could hear. I was happy that Nathan had dozed off because the slightest whimper or cry from him would've blown my cover.

"Hummer's mom went to the cops to file a missing persons report on him," Tyrell informed. "No one has heard from him since the week after the frat party."

"Y'all know how Hummer is, man," Germaine responded. "He's probably locked away with a few freaks doing only God knows what."

"You may be right, but he usually calls somebody to boast about it."

"I know. He's gonna turn up somewhere just give him a few more days," Germaine added.

When the conversation shifted to the wedding, I retreated to my upstairs office. I needed to call Kingston and let him know what was going on. But before I could get the chance to make that call, Johnathan ran into my office soaking wet from the pool.

"Mommy, daddy tol' me to tell you to dry me off," he said, dripping water all over my plush tan carpet.

"John John, stop slinging water everywhere!" I yelled while trying to press the number two button on my phone for Kingston.

Instantly, Nathan woke up from his catnap crying.

"Mommy, I'm cold. Mommy, Nathan stinks. Did he boo boo," Johnathan continued, making me wish that I'd gone to the studio.

"John John, hush!"

I put the cell up to my ear then dropped it along with my mouth when I heard the operator inform me that the line had been disconnected.

"Mommy, I'm cold!" Johnathan whined between shivers.

Before I knew it, I slapped my son across the face which caused him to start crying immediately.

"Will you please just shut the hell up?!" I screamed.

The chaos of Kingston's phone being turned off, Johnathan whining and Nathan crying struck a nerve and I screamed to the top of my lungs. Seconds later, I could hear footsteps racing up the stairs sounding like a herd of horses. Germaine and Tyrell rushed into my office.

"What happened?" Germaine panicked. After running

over to me and inspecting Nathan, he glanced to see if Johnathan was okay.

"Take him! Please!" I begged then shoved Nathan into his arms.

"Nikki, what in the hell is the matter with you?"

I hopped out of my chair. "I need to lay down."

"Germaine, I'll get up with you later," Tyrell said realizing that it was probably best that he leave.

"You don't have to leave, Tyrell," I addressed before he walked out. "I'll leave."

I started toward the door, but Germaine grabbed my arm and pushed me back into my chair.

"Sit your ass back down," he growled. His forehead wrinkled and eyebrows connected to show that he was pissed.

I could tell that Tyrell was really uncomfortable and didn't want to be a part of what was about to go down.

"I'm out, Germaine," Tyrell said as he started toward the door again.

"Okay, Ty. I'll holla, man."

After hearing the front door open and close, Germaine tore into me.

"What in the fuck is wrong with you?" he barked.

"No, what the fuck is wrong with you?" I quickly turned the tables. "You're getting a little bit too damn comfortable putting your hands on me."

"Fuck that! Did you hit John John?"

"Yeah. He was getting on my nerves so I hit his ass."

"John John, go in the bathroom, take off your trunks and get a towel to dry off," Germaine addressed our son whose teeth were now chattering.

Johnathan did as he was told and raced to the bathroom. Germaine stared at me as if he were waiting for an explanation. If that was the case, his ass would be waiting forever because I wasn't about to give him one. The man that I wanted was no longer available to me and I didn't know why. I wondered if it was because of the kiss he saw me sharing with Germaine or the fact that he realized he truly loved his wife and wanted to be with her. Whatever the case, I needed to know. I wanted to know. I had to know.

Germaine stood in silence as he tried to figure out what was going on with me. No matter how hard he tried, he would and could never figure it out. However, when I thought about the way I'd just reacted, I knew my actions must've frightened my sons. I didn't want that and I needed for them to know how sorry I was. I definitely needed Johnathan to know that I was sorry because I'd never hit him before. I reached for Nathan, but Germaine pulled him back.

"I don't know what your problem is, Nikki, but you need to get your shit together," Germaine scolded. "Nathan has had this dirty diaper on for nearly thirty minutes and you haven't attempted to change him yet. When you're home, be home. That's all we ask. You need to leave that other shit at the door or at the damn studio."

"I have my shit together," I retaliated.

"I can't tell." He handed Nathan back to me.

"I thought you were going to change him?" I questioned.

"Be your kids' mother. You take care of them for a change. I'm meeting Tyrell and the boys for some last minute wedding stuff. If you have any problems, call 9-1-1," Germaine mocked then walked out leaving me speechless. "And if you hit my son again, that'll be your last time," he added before walking out.

"This nigga has lost his fucking mind," I growled under my breath as I powered up my laptop. The diaper change would just have to wait once again.

When I clicked on the folder named *Dream,* four photos of houses opened up. I couldn't wait to show Kingston the houses in Modesto, California, Durham, North Carolina, Newport, Virginia and Sarasota, Florida. I wanted us to choose together which one of them we would live in. He's never come straight out and told me that he wanted us to be together, but his actions spoke louder than his words. *Why else would he kill for me*? No man who didn't love his woman would do such a thing.

I smiled as I closed each picture. Before I stood up, I noticed an icon flashing on my laptop to let me know that I had a new email message. I clicked on it, opened the mailbox and gasped when new photos of me and Kingston popped up.

"Fuck! Who in the hell could be following us?"

Agitated, annoyed and slightly afraid, I rocked Nathan a little harder causing the stench to fill the air. I knew that I needed to get the ball rolling a little faster before I was exposed and had to give Germaine half of my money.

Days had passed and I still hadn't heard from Kingston. I was pissed and confused because his actions were totally uncalled for. The following Friday night, I was sitting behind my desk at the label thinking about Kingston as usual. His absence and fucked up attitude was driving me crazy. Each time my phone rung, I would get pissed when it wasn't him. I was a mess and it was all because of his ass.

My door was slightly ajar when I heard a few of my producers walk by. They were discussing what club they were gonna hit after they finished laying tracks and listening to demos from two new artists, Dizzy and Flex, I hoped to sign. My boys were with my mother for the weekend and I didn't give a damn about Germaine's whereabouts. It was time that I had me some fun and I knew exactly who to call. I had my fingers crossed that he hadn't left town yet.

"Does that offer still stand?" I asked A.J. when he answered. There was loud laughter in the background.

"What?" he yelled over the noise. "Hold on! Let me go somewhere a little quieter!" I waited for a few seconds before he returned. "Niquole, is that you?"

"Yeah, it's me. I need to see you." I didn't have time to play games.

"What?"

"You heard me. Are you still in Houston?"

"Yeah."

"Where are you?!"

"I'm at Dave & Buster's on Richmond."

"Can I see you?"

"You know you can," A.J. replied. "Would you rather meet me at my hotel? I'm at the Doubletree downtown on Dallas Street."

"No, stay where you are."

"Okay. You want me to order some wings or something?"

"Naw, I have an appetite for something else."

I hung up and grabbed my purse. There was no need for me to sit at my desk doing nothing especially when I couldn't talk to Kingston. I closed and locked my door then headed out.

I called A.J. as soon as I arrived at the adult Chuck-E-Cheese twenty minutes later. He answered on the first ring. "You're here?"

"I'm walking through now. Where are you?" I asked.

"I'm at the bar."

"I'll be there in a sec."

The place was crowded, but I eventually made my way to the bar. I spotted A.J. sitting on a stool tossing back a shot and chatting it up with a few guys. As I walked toward him, the guys he was talking to immediately eyed me from head to toe. A.J.'s back was turned so he didn't see me.

"So, you got a shot for me?" I whispered in A.J.'s ear.

He swung around and smiled at me. "Damn! You look good," he gawked. I was wearing a pair of black leggings, a gray oversized top and some studded Valentino sandals. "What are you drinking?" he asked before gesturing for the waiter.

I leaned into his ear again then nibbled on the lobe. "Let's get out of here and I'll show you."

Five seconds hadn't even passed before A.J. placed twenty bucks on the counter then hopped off the stool. "It's been real boys, but booty calls. I mean duty," he addressed the guys before we walked off. "So, what do I owe this pleasure or better yet, who's pissed you off?" he asked when we made it to his rental.

"Does it matter?"

He smiled. "It never has."

"Then shut up and get me out of here."

"Yes, ma'am." Once we got in the car, A.J. cranked the 2009, white, Dodge Charger then backed out of the parking space and drove off. "I knew you'd call," he said with confidence. He was so full of himself, but he had ten thick, mind-blowing reasons to be.

"I knew I would, too," I replied wishing he'd press the gas a little more.

"Miss Niquole. Miss Niquole," he sang while cutting his eyes at me. "Just couldn't stay away, huh?"

I could do without the small talk. I just needed him to help me get Kingston off my brain. I needed to shut him up and I wasn't waiting until we got to his hotel. "Pull over."

"Pull over? For what?"

I lifted my top up then pulled my breast out of my beige and chocolate half-bra. "You wanna wait 'til you get to the hotel to taste these?"

A.J. damn near hit the car that was on the side of us when he jerked to pull over. When we made it to the shoulder, he eagerly placed the car in park. "I see you still got that freak in you," he said before reaching over and adjusting my seat so that it was back as far as it could go. "I'm always that fucking remedy, huh?" he breathed on my chest after climbing on top of me.

I ignored him and slithered out of my leggings after unbuckling then kicking off my shoes. I wanted Kingston off my mind and I knew I was moments away from getting my wish.

A.J. teased my nipples with his tongue. He knew that drove me crazy. To intensify the pleasure he was already giving me, he slipped two fingers inside my wetness.

"Damn, girl. You already wet."

"That's all you," I said in his ear. I think I excited him when I eased two of my fingers inside my pussy as well to assist him with the finger fuck.

"You a bad girl, Niquole…a bad girl."

"Then punish me."

I guess those were the words he was waiting to hear. "We need to get in the back seat, baby," A.J. said before opening the passenger door. He climbed out first and I was a few steps behind him. A few cars passed by, but no one was the wiser or they pretended not to be. He opened the back door and we quickly dipped inside.

"Come on, A.J. Stop playing with me," I begged while helping him undo his pants.

"I'm coming, baby. I'm coming."

He pulled a condom front his front pocket, ripped off the wrapper and rolled it on. Seconds later, Kingston was temporarily the farthest thing from my mind. I wasted no time thrusting when he was inside.

"Damn! Shit, Work that pussy like you used to, baby!"

I thrust and rolled keeping up with every stab that he gave me. A.J. lifted up a little and grabbed the driver's side headrest to hold him up while he hammered me. My fingers soon assisted.

"A.J., oooooh! Damn!"

"I got you, baby. I hear ya."

My left leg was soon in the crease of his arm. I bit the inside of my lip because his slow roll was to kill for. I hated that we ended on bad terms because our sex together was dynamic. We both were selfish, greedy and secretive. Speaking of secrets, only a handful of people knew about the one that we shared.

"A.J., right there baby! Right there! Don't you move! Don't you dare fucking move!" I coached him when he hit the spot.

"I know what I'm doing, baby," he replied conceitedly.

He lay in my pussy and rolled…then jabbed...rolled…then jabbed. I couldn't take it anymore. My body began twitching like I was having an epileptic seizure. My eyes rolled to the back of my head, but he didn't stop. He continued to roll…then jab.

"A.J., you've got to stop," I begged and fought to break free, but he had a crucial lock on my leg. If I had kicked that window any harder, I'm sure he would be replacing it.

"Another one's coming right?" he asked already knowing the answer.

My body answered for me as it jerked and twitched. He knew it so well. I howled like a wolf at the moon.

"Let's take this back to my hotel so I can give it to you how you really want it," he suggested with warm breath against my ear.

How in the hell was I going to say no to that?

I entered my house nearly four the next morning. I was floating, and A.J. had rocked my damn world. I didn't even want to leave, but knew I had to. Germaine blew my phone up for nearly an hour until A.J. turned it off. Having A.J. inside of me would be worth the fight that I knew I'd be walking into. I hoped Germaine would be passed out when I got home, but that wish was never granted.

I walked to the kitchen for a glass of water. My throat was parched from the loud moaning and screaming. The neighbors definitely knew his name. I finished off the water in a matter of seconds then placed the glass in the sink and headed for the staircase. When I reached them and looked up, Germaine was standing at the top glaring down at me.

"Where have you been?" he asked harshly.

"Where in the hell you think?" I barked back.

"It's almost four in the morning, Nikki."

"And? I've stayed later than this at the studio before," I shot back.

"Why didn't you answer your phone? Better yet, why did you turn it off?"

I really didn't feel like doing this back and forth shit with him. I needed to lay down and get some sleep. "I was in the studio. I couldn't be disturbed," I lied then slowly climbed the stairs. I damn near tripped as I walked up.

"Drunk, huh?" he asked after seeing me stumble.

Yeah. Drunk off of cum, I thought. "I'm not like you, Germaine. I don't drink to get drunk."

He gave me one last glare then turned to walk away. "I hope you didn't forget Tyrell's wedding tomorrow."

"How could I? You talk about it every day."

"It must be raining outside?" he changed the subject.

"No. Why?" I asked curiously.

"Because your hair is a little wet."

I stared at him while holding a straight face as I touched the ends of my hair. He was right. I forced back that smile that was fighting to come through as I thought back to the shower with A.J.

"Look, it's late. We can do this shit later." I continued up the stairs hoping he wouldn't ask any more questions regarding my appearance. I had no answers for him even if he did.

I stood at the buffet table at the Ayva Center with a frown on my face then turned up my nose and shook my head. What in the hell was I doing at this ghetto-ass reception? I should've known it would be just as ghetto as the wedding. The church was small, hot and packed like a can of sardines. I even had to leave and sit in my car. As hot as it was, I definitely wasn't going to let the heat ruin my hair, makeup and outfit. The look that Germaine gave me as he stood next to Tyrell at the alter was death defying, but of course I didn't give a damn. I needed air.

I assumed Tyrell and his new bride couldn't afford to have the reception professionally catered after kicking out the rental fee for the center. They should've asked some of those frat brothers that Germaine spoke so highly of to pitch in because this shit was a disaster. Anyone and everyone had pitched in on cooking the food.

"What you want?"

I looked up at the greasy faced, chunky woman and fought back my laughter. This heifer had gold and purple weave in her head, about twenty gold necklaces around her neck and gold and purple nails. She clutched the spoon in her hand like she was a skilled chef. Did her ghetto ass really think she was about to serve me some food?

"I think I'll pass," I stated then walked off.

"Whatever," she responded.

The gold and purple decorations were just as awful. Well, they were okay, but the decorator did a terrible job piecing it all together. Meagan would've showed her ass off if she had her hand in the event. Then it hit me. These were ghetto folks, and ghetto folks did ghetto things like buying cheap paper plates and cups, and not having enough food to feed everyone. Not only did I see a couple of guys bringing in coolers, but there were even a couple of instances where a few females were about to tussle with their baby's daddies. It was a mess and I didn't fit in…at all.

It didn't take long for the chaos to cease when the DJ announced Tyrell and his lovely bride. She looked a hot mess in her ancient looking wedding dress. She must've dug that shit out of her grandmother's closet and had one of her ghetto friends try and spiff it up. I wanted to take a picture and post it on You Tube, but just decided to laugh it off.

Whoever coordinated their wedding also did a horrible job. For one, the bride and groom should've hit the dance floor before any of their guests. Now, the DJ had to clear the guests off the floor so the bride and groom could have their first dance.

"I know good and damn well this mofo is not playing *Shake That Ass Bitch* by Splack Pack?" I mumbled to myself. The crowd roared and cheered as Tyrell and his bride cut a rug on the floor. "I can't believe this," I laughed under my breath. That fiasco went on for nearly ten minutes.

I was so happy when all of the frat *dogs* raced to the dance floor for a step show because it gave me a moment to myself. I wanted to get away from the loud, colorful guests. No one wore an outfit that cost over fifty dollars and they probably got a discount on that price. I noticed the eyes staring and noses tooting up at me because I had that *I'm the shit* look on my face and stance. There was no need to deny it, I was. I was the best looking thing in the room and they knew it.

Roberto Cavalli should've paid me for looking so damn good in the draped, halter dress that I kicked out two grand for the occasion. I needed to let these people know what a real woman looked like.

After the ten minute step show, the men reclaimed their women. I assumed some of them must've forgotten that they'd left their stamina back in college because they were panting and sweating like real dogs.

"You okay?" Germaine asked when he found me at the buffet table shaking my head at the food. I was really hungry, so I decided to suck it up and grab something. The ghetto server had left the table unattended so I could pick through what I wanted.

"I'm good," I replied before tossing a meatball in my mouth then spitting it back out in the plate I was holding. It tasted worse that it looked. Knowing I couldn't go wrong with fried chicken since it was comfort food for black people, I tried that next. "Decent," I said out loud.

"Hey man," Tyrell interrupted, "the groomsmen are about to take pictures."

Wow, shouldn't they have done that already? I thought. *This wedding is ass backwards*.

"Oh, okay," Germaine addressed Tyrell who didn't move. I guess he wanted to make sure that Germaine was going to follow him. Germaine leaned in my ear so that Tyrell wouldn't hear what he was about to say. "Please come out front with me," he whined.

I held back my laughter because he sounded so pathetic. I never understood why he allowed me to treat him like shit and continued to stay with me. I wondered if he had some type of ulterior motive because I would've left my ass a long time ago. That night at the album release party would've been the breaking point for me if the roles were reversed.

"Nikki, please," Germaine whispered again.

I took a deep breath and nodded at him. He

smiled…hard.

When we walked toward the lobby, I could feel the stares on me. Next, came all the snickers. I even heard one trick tell another that she heard I was crying in the bathroom at the album release party. At that moment I instantly thought back to the two females who I cursed out in the restroom. I could only imagine how far that gossip had spread. As much as I wanted to go off on their asses, I kept my cool.

As soon as we made it to the front lobby, my fingers went numb and the plate I was holding hit the floor.

"Are you okay?" Germaine asked when he saw my stiffened body and the terrified look on my face.

"I need the groom and the groomsmen on the steps, please," the photographer spoke.

I snapped out of my terrified stupor when I heard the short, chubby, dark-skinned photographer address the wedding party.

"Nikki? Nikki?"

"What?" I snapped at Germaine.

Before he could respond, Tyrell had called out to him to hurry up for the photos. He walked away with a curious look on his face. After he left, I turned to Kingston.

What in the hell was he doing at the reception? I thought.

When he rolled his eyes at me, I knew he was still pissed that I'd kissed Germaine at the party. Even though I was only doing it to make him jealous, by his actions, it seemed to have worked. I smiled at him when he looked at me. Again, he rolled his eyes.

His chocolate ass looked so damn good in the light-grey Hugo Boss shirt and charcoal slacks. I glanced around the lobby to see if there was anywhere he and I could disappear to. I had to have him. I wanted him…bad. I needed to be near him. I needed to smell him.

As I was about to make my move, I halted my steps and

gasped as I watched the figure bounce from the other end of the lobby and into Kingston's arms. I glanced at her attire and realized she was part of the wedding party and she was the same bitch from the party…his wife. I immediately fumed.

"You're done already, baby," I heard him ask her.

"Yes," she answered before leaning in to kiss him. He grabbed and squeezed her ass. That son-of-a-bitch knew that I was watching. "Stop that," she laughed then playfully pushed his hand away. "Save that for later." I'd reached my fucking boiling point.

My mind raced as I asked myself over and over what her connection could be to Tyrell or his bride since she was in the wedding party. The whole thing was odd and confusing.

"Do y'all think it's appropriate to be doing that out here?" I addressed them once they started to tongue each other down. I tried to disguise the anger in my voice.

She glared at me then turned back to Kingston who was giving me the same expression.

"Come on. Let's dance," she suggested to him after rolling her eyes at me. She grabbed Kingston's hand and pulled him back inside the reception area before he could agree. Of course, I followed them inside.

I lurked amongst the guests as I watched the two of them grind and slobber all over each other. I knew he was aware that I was somewhere watching and just wanted to piss me off or pay me back from the other night. But I couldn't take it. I eased through the crowd like a slimy snake until I reached them. Mary J. Blige's *Just Fine* had filled the room and I watched as that bitch threw her ass on my man. Kingston poured more salt on my wound by grabbing the front of her thighs and pulling her back to him so that he could grind on her ass. Before I stormed off the floor, I bumped into them. On purpose of course.

"I'm sorry," his wife apologized as if it were her fault and not the other way around. She didn't even bother to look up. I wanted to spit in that bitch's face. When Kingston stared at me, I walked off.

A few minutes later, my cell phone vibrated. I pulled it out of my purse and read the text message: ***Don't try that shit again***. I knew it was from Kingston so I stored his new number in my phone.

I had to get your attention somehow since you're ignoring me!!! Why did you change your number? *I replied.*

I don't play second fiddle to no man, *was his response.*

I smiled because that was confirmation that he was jealous. ***That's not fair. You kissed your wife in front of me.***

You can't do what I do, he replied.

I looked up from my Blackberry and spotted Kingston walking off the dance floor. I quickly replied: ***Baby, I'm sorry. I love you. I want us to be together. Just let me know what I need to do to make that happen? Meet me outside. I want you***.

After pressing the send button, I looked up and watched him read my plea. I was a little confused when I saw a sly smile form on his face and he slipped his phone in his pocket without replying. I couldn't understand why he was playing games with me. I needed answers and I was gonna get them.

Before I had a chance to cross his path, a woman started screaming causing the entire party to come at a standstill. I followed the crowd that gathered around her.

"Not my baby! No! Lord, not my baby!" the middle aged, woman screamed.

"What's going on?' I asked the guy standing next to me.

"She just found out that her son is dead," he answered. "Hummer was a cool dude. He didn't…"

"Did you just say Hummer?" I asked frighteningly.

"Yeah."

I slowly backed out of the crowd until I spotted Kingston who was smiling heartily. Then he did the unthinkable.

"Didn't he fuck around with other men's women? One of them probably killed him," Kingston blurted out.

Mouths dropped and eyes bucked including mine. I knew I could be insensitive sometimes, but that shit was downright cruel. Especially since he was the one who actually ended the man's life. The crowd showed their disapproval by cursing him out. However, it didn't seem to bother him one bit. As Kingston walked away from the mob, I spotted his wife in a corner trying to hide the fact that she was crying, too. Again, I questioned how she knew Tyrell and now Hummer, of course. *Damn, I wonder if she knows Germaine, too*?

"We need to get out of here," Germaine startled me from behind.

I turned to him. His eyes were red as fire and filled with tears. I knew he wanted me to comfort and console him, but I couldn't. I was the reason why his friend was dead.

"You want me to drive?" I offered.

He gave me a cold look, reached inside his pocket and handed me the keys. We flowed with the weeping crowd and exited the building. Once outside, I spotted Kingston and his wife talking. He lifted her chin and pecked her on the lips when he saw me staring at them. Then he went in for the kill. That tongue that I wanted down my throat was traveling down hers.

"Bastard," I said loudly enough for him to hear.

"What did you say?" Germaine asked.

Without answering, I hightailed it to my car. As soon as I was within a few feet, all I could do was laugh when I saw all four of my tires flat on the ground.

"Jealous bitches," I replied then smiled.

My grin quickly diminished when I realized that it could've been the person blackmailing me. I wasn't sure, but either way, I needed to involve Kingston. I retrieved my cell phone to text him but Germaine's presence stopped that.

"What the hell? Are you calling AAA?" he asked.

"Aww…yeah," I stammered knowing that wasn't the reason my phone was in my hand.

Around three a.m., I jumped up from my desk after briefly dozing off. I had a dream about me being in jail because of Hummer's death and my involvement in it. I was dressed in scrubs surrounded by a bunch of butch lesbians waiting to take their turns with me. A light bulb went off in my head as I regrouped from the dream. I still hadn't gotten rid of the jacket even though my intentions were to. When I left the office that day, I placed the bag in my trunk and planned to toss it in a dumpster on the way home, but it started raining which ultimately distracted my mission.

I tiptoed down the carpeted stairs with my keys clutched tightly in my hand making sure they didn't make a sound. Once in the kitchen, I disabled the alarm and walked out the side door. Luckily, I didn't have to disturb the garage door. I popped the trunk of my car and snatched the Target bag out before walking toward the back of the house where the two garbage bins were. Quickly looking over my shoulder, I lifted one of the tops and held my breath as the stench brushed past my nose. There were two garbage bags inside. I tore one of them open and shoved the Target bag deep inside. When I pulled my arm out, it was covered with bread crumbs, apple peels and a few strands of spaghetti. I wanted to curse, but knew Germaine would hear me from his bedroom window. After picking up a leaf from the ground and flicking the garbage off of my arm, I closed the lid. I thought everything had worked out until I glanced at the upstairs window and saw the panels moving back and forth. Nervously placing my freshly done nail inside my mouth, I hoped like hell that it was just the AC turning back on.

A week after the reception, I drove through my gated community admiring the bomb ass job that La-lien had done on my nails. If I didn't know they were acrylic, I would've mistaken them for the real thing. Kingston was still giving me the silent treatment, but truthfully it should've been the other way around. He was the one acting like a fucking teenager and kissing his wife in front of me. I was pissed, and I wanted to voice it to him. He needed to know how I felt.

Seconds later, I pulled into my yard and came to an abrupt stop when I saw that Germaine's truck was parked on the lawn. He had lost his mind. *I paid over two grand for that grass to look like that.*

"His stupid ass knows better than this," I fumed before gliding out of my car and storming inside the house. "Germaine! Germaine! Where in the hell are you? You need to get that truck off my grass before you fuck it up!" I shouted before searching the house for him.

Eventually, I found him in the basement or better known as his could-have-been-studio. He was playing some tunes on his Yamaha keyboard while tapping on his beat machine at the same time. I hadn't been down in the basement in so long that I'd completely forgotten that the old ass equipment was there. He needed an upgrade, but I wasn't about to give him money for it.

"You need to move your truck off the grass, Germaine. I paid a lot of money for that grass."

"I know what the fuck…you paid for. I… was with you when you picked it out," he slurred before turning up the Grey Goose bottle. I glanced down at his feet and saw a few beer bottles as well. His ass was drunk. "Where are the boys?"

"What the fuck do you care? You're never here anyway."

"Fuck you, Germaine. I hope you get sclerosis of the fucking liver."

I turned and walked back upstairs. My boys were nowhere to be found, so I assumed they were with his folks. He normally didn't get hammered when they were around. Plus, I'm sure he wanted to sulk in his own damn misery.

"Why won't you go with me to Hummer's funeral?" he startled me after I walked out of the kitchen a few minutes later.

I stepped away from him because he was all in my face with his rancid breath. The combination of alcohol and cigarettes didn't sit too well with me.

"You already know that I'll be in New Orleans checking out some new talent so, I don't know why you fixed your mouth to ask me that," I said, before walking down the stairs. He was close on my heels.

"Isn't that what you pay people for?"

"Yes, but I'm going and you know why. But if all of the alcohol that you consume has warped your brain, let me refresh your memory."

"No need."

"Good."

He knew good and damn well why I was going. I loved being part of the scouting. I loved seeing the talent and the hunger in their eyes. It reminded me of when I used to be in their shoes chasing record deals.

"Can't you fly out after the funeral?" he whined.

"No, I can't."

"That's fucked up, Nikki. Hummer was my fucking friend."

"You're correct. He was *your* friend," I concurred then pointed at him in case he'd forgotten. "He was your friend…not mine. Furthermore, the son-of-a-bitch tried to rape me. I wouldn't dare offer my respects to him. As far as I'm concerned he can rot in hell because that's where he's going."

"Can you be there for me, Nikki? Please."

I stepped away from him, stared into his eyes and gave him a very disapproving look. He was weak and he needed to know that.

"Your friend deserved to die for what he tried to do to me and there's no telling how many other women he's raped. I'm not going to that fucking funeral. Not for you or any one else! How can you sit up here and ask me that shit? You're weak and a sorry ass excuse for a man!"

I shocked him when I didn't flinch after he threw his beer bottle. It barely missed my head before it hit the wall and shattered. Seconds later, Germaine jumped in my face and raised his hand as to slap me. I was ready to call his bluff.

"Hit me! Hit me like you should've hit Hummer when he stuck his finger in my pussy!" I taunted. I wanted him to hit me. I wanted a bruise on my face so that I could run to Kingston crying. I was more than sure he wouldn't let it slide.

I watched Germaine bite down on his lip and slowly lower his hand. "Sorry ass," I chuckled sinisterly in his face, but stopped when he spit in mine. I was frozen as I watched him stumble toward the door and open it.

"You haven't fucked me in damn near a year," he slurred. "You would think that you'd do that much for me."

"You need to ask yourself why I haven't fucked you," I snarled at him still shocked by his actions and words.

"If I ain't hittin' it, I'm sure another nigga is," he growled back.

"And I'm sure you're getting pussy from somewhere since I haven't been fucking you," I retaliated.

"When you love someone, you don't do that type of shit, Nikki."

I jumped when he slammed the door. Shaking my head in disbelief, I wiped the glob of spit that was trickling down my eye. The engine on his truck revving brought me out of my shock. I listened to his tires screech as he zoomed down the street. I prayed that he ran into a fucking telephone pole.

Stomping up the stairs like a mad woman, I shoved the bathroom door open, stood in front of the marble sink and stared at myself in the mirror. I was pissed. I grabbed the bottle of liquid Dove soap, lathered it up then rubbed it all over my face. After ridding my skin of his spit, I flew into my room and called Kingston. No answer.

I sat at my desk and waited five minutes before calling again. Still, no answer. I stared at the luggage that I'd packed for my trip to New Orleans. There was no way that I was gonna be home when Germaine got back. Instantly, I jumped out of the chair, grabbed the bag and dashed out the door. I frowned when I saw the tire marks that his dumb ass had left on my lawn. After angrily tossing the bag in the trunk of my car, I climbed inside and drove off.

Nearly thirty minutes later, I checked into the Hyatt Regency on Louisiana Street in downtown Houston. As soon as I made it to my room, I sat down on the comfortable bed and dialed Germaine's mother's number. I really didn't want to talk to that wench, but I wanted to check on my boys.

"Are my boys with you?" I wasted no time when she answered.

"First of all, you're not going to call my house with a damn attitude and not speak," she quickly shot back.

I hated listening to her wanna-be proper ass talk because it was all fake. She eliminated her New Orleans drawl as soon as she moved to Houston three years ago.

I ignored her. "Bitch, are my boys with you?"

Before she could go off on me again, I heard Johnathan in the background laughing as well as Nathan cooing. I figured she must've been holding him. At that moment, I hung up the phone in her face. All I needed to know was where they were.

Thinking back to Kingston, I couldn't deal with this silent treatment he was giving me. After clicking on the television, there was a knock at the door.

"Who in the hell could this be?" I mumbled. When I opened the door I nearly lost my balance as I stared at one-hundred and seventy-five pounds of butterscotch. He had to have the wrong room.

"May I help you?" I asked.

"Ms. Wright, you left your ID at the front desk."

I extended my hand to retrieve the card. "Thank you. I'd truly be lost without this," I smiled.

He returned the smile. "You seemed a little distracted downstairs. We all make mistakes."

Was this six foot stallion paying that much attention to me downstairs? He stood so sure of himself in his black suit. His name tag read: *Darren, Manager.*

"Well, I'm sorry for the trouble, Darren."

"No trouble at all, ma'am."

Little did he know, I wanted to get into some trouble with him. "Darren, let me give you something for coming all the way up here," I said walking back inside the room.

"Oh, no, ma'am. I can't accept anything from you. It's my job to make sure that all guests have a pleasant experience while staying here." I wondered what he was thinking when I didn't respond. "Ma'am? Ms. Wright?"

His eyes widened when I returned to the door. I was standing in my baby blue, Victoria's Secret, bra and panty set. "Can you accept this?" I asked seductively.

He tugged at his tie. I guess things were getting a little too hot for him, but he didn't pass up the offer. He walked inside and closed the door. “This is a first for me,” he said like he’d entered a strip club for the first time.

“Me too,” I lied.

I walked up to him and removed his jacket then rubbed and squeezed all over his pecs. He was just enough man, if not more, to get Kingston off my brain. I stared into his eyes while I slowly unbuttoned his stiff, white shirt. His chest poked out like a Spartan. I could tell that the gym was his friend. The four-inch, Dior platform pumps were not high enough for me to reach his lips. Instead, I gently pulled his face to mine. I air kissed him for a few seconds. I felt his breath on my lips as I continued to tease him. Obviously, he couldn’t take it. Darren grabbed my arm and swung me around.

“I shouldn’t be doing this,” he said while kissing my neck. “I’m married.”

“So am I,” I spoke softly.

My response must’ve done something to him because Darren tasted my body from my neck all the way down to my ass. He then gripped the sides of my panties and snatched them down like they didn’t belong.

“Mmmmmmm,” I moaned. In those few seconds, Kingston was gone. I opened my legs a little wider to allow his fingers access into my pussy. “Mmmmmmm,” I moaned again when they were inside. “Ooooooooh!” I grabbed my breast and squeezed them.

He crawled in front of me before lifting my leg and carefully placing it over his shoulder. His dark brown eyes stayed locked on mine. He was seconds away from going in for the kill.

“Darren, we need you downstairs,” were the words that suddenly came through his walkie talkie.

I obviously wasn’t going to get the chance of experiencing that oral. I wanted to grab that two-way radio and throw it across the room. He rested his head on my ass for a minute then took a deep breath. I was just as disappointed as he was because Kingston was slowly reentering my mind.

"Perfect timing, huh?" he joked. "I'm getting off in a couple of hours. Can I come back later?" he asked after standing up and slipping on his jacket.

My buzz had been killed. "That may not be a good idea."

He seemed a little disappointed, but hey, it was what it was. He had to catch me while I was in the moment. After going to the bathroom and washing his hands, he left.

Sadly, I spent the next few hours calling Kingston only to be disappointed. I listened to his entire voice message each time just so I could hear his voice. Thinking about him and listening to his voice had aroused me. My nipples hardened and my pussy moistened. I was in bed naked so I had easy access to them.

"Mmmmmm, Kingston," I spoke into the phone after the recorder allowed me to leave a message. My hands massaged my breasts then eagerly eased between my legs to help my water fountain flow. "Baby…..mmmmmmm….it's wet for you, baby. She wants you." I placed the phone between my legs to let him hear me fingering myself. "You hear that, baby?" I spoke into the phone after pressing it back against my ear. "She needs you, baby." The only thing that I loved about masturbating was the fact that I knew my spots. "Kingston, you're about to make me cum, baby! Baby! Baby!" I howled before dropping the phone.

Seconds later, my balloon popped. "Shit, that was a good one," I said to myself before picking the phone back up. After calling back and getting his voice mail once again, I left one final message. "I love you, baby and I'm sorry. I'll make it up to you. I promise."

I fell asleep with the phone still glued to my ear.

Chapter Fourteen

I stepped off the plane at the Louis Armstrong New Orleans International Airport and high stepped to the baggage claim to collect my bags. Once that task was done, I dashed outside and through the slew of people. I needed to catch the first available cab to my hotel. I was extremely pissed that I had to catch a damn cab in the first place. I tore into Meagan as soon as she called to inform me that there was a mix up with the car service. I hung up the phone in her beautifully tanned face and took two deep, long breaths before walking out the door and into the crowded entranceway. For the amount of time I spent trying to hail a cab, I could've rented a damn car and drove to the hotel. You would think that the cabbies knew money when they saw it. I figured if I was dressed in a white t-shirt, skinny jeans, dreads bunched up under a ball cap and skin inked all over then they would've flocked to me. But unfortunately I didn't look like Lil' Wayne. Little did they know, I was money. I reached into my Chanel purse, pulled out a hundred dollar bill and waved it in the air. It was at that moment when three cabs finally raced to me.

"Good afternoon, ma'am," the freckle faced white man addressed me after hopping out of the driver's seat. The cab smelled just like fresh pine.

"Whatever," I replied. "Take me to the W Hotel on Poydras," I continued before placing the money back inside my purse. His facial expression told me that he knew he'd been swindled.

I pulled my phone out of my purse and called A.J. I needed a fix.

"Damn, girl, it hasn't been a year yet," he joked after answering.

I laughed. "I'm in town."

"Oh really?" I could hear the excitement in his voice.

"I'm staying at the W on Poydras. I'll call you with the room number."

"Now, how do you know I don't have anything to do?"

"I'm sure you'd rather be *doing* me instead," I said before hanging up.

While the cabbie drove the few miles to the hotel, the incident between me and Germaine weighed heavy on my mind. I still couldn't believe that he spit in my face. Even though I still hadn't been back home since everything went down, he was surely gonna pay for that shit. My mother was curious to know why I'd called and asked her to check on the boys. But I didn't give her a reason. I just demanded that she do so.

Germaine rang my cell phone off the hook leaving messages apologizing, wanting to know my whereabouts and blaming the alcohol for his behavior. All he needed to know was that I was pissed. It hurt me not to see my boys for those two days, but I knew they were in good hands. Being in the hotel gave me time to clear my head and think. Germaine may've thought he was in hell before, but that was just the beginning. He would pay in due time.

When the cab driver dropped me off at the hotel, I handed him fifteen bucks. He fumed because it wasn't the hundred that I'd originally waved to him. After dropping my luggage on the ground, he angrily sped away to see if he could make up for the loss. Not giving a damn, I walked through the hotel lobby as if I owned it and didn't have a care in the world.

"Welcome to the W. Are you checking in today?" the cheerful, brunette front desk clerk greeted me.

"Yes, I have a reservation under Niquole Wright."

"Don't you own a record label? I've seen you in a few magazines," she said. I could tell that she was waiting for me to say yes, but I wasn't in the mood to have a conversation.

"No, and I'm getting tired of people mistaking me for her."

"Oh, I'm sorry," she apologized and turned to her computer. She knew that I was lying.

While she tapped her keyboard, I fumbled around in my purse for my platinum American Express. When I located it, I handed her the card along with my ID.

"Non smoking, king bed, please," I requested.

"Of course Ms. Wright. No problem."

I liked the sound of Ms. Wright as opposed to Mrs.

She tapped the keyboard a little more before swiping my credit card. "I hope you enjoy your stay, Ms. Wright," she smiled after handing me everything back, including my room key. "I love your label."

I couldn't help but smile.

Once I called A.J. to give him the room number, I rolled my luggage to the elevator and up to the seventh floor. After sliding the keycard in the slot on the door and opening it, I stood in the threshold when I heard the water in the bathroom running. I glanced in the hall and didn't see a maid's cleaning cart, so I wondered who was in my room.

"Hello?" I spoke loudly. I glanced over my room receipt then back at the number on the door. They matched. "I think you've got the wrong room!" Wondering what the hell was going on, I jumped when the bathroom door opened and Kingston appeared.

"What are you doing here?" I instantly ran up to him and after threw my arms around his neck. He didn't return the embrace, but my arms stayed put. "How did you know I'd be here?"

"You left me so many damn messages the other night. You don't remember telling me where you would be?" he asked with a pissed off look on his face.

I removed my arms "I hope you're not mad," I whimpered. "I just wanted to hear your voice."

"Whatever," he replied nonchalantly and walked over to the window.

He was still pissed and obviously I'd made it worse. *Maybe his wife questioned him about the calls and he had to lie about them,* I thought. I needed to make things right. I walked over to him and hesitantly placed my hands on his shoulders.

"I'm sorry, baby," I whispered softly in his ear. "What can I do to fix this?"

He didn't move or speak a word as I slipped my hands under his shirt and began massaging his back. When I reached his shoulders, he walked away. I knew this was going to be hard work, but I was willing to put in the time. I sat down on the king sized bed, removed my sandals then looked up at him.

"Why did you even come here to surprise me if you're gonna just stand there and not say anything?" I asked getting a little ticked off. "I don't understand why you're so pissed off at me." Before he could even respond, it finally dawned on me. "Hold up…how did you even get the room number?"

"I paid the white girl downstairs a hefty fee to set everything up," Kingston replied.

Maybe he does love me. I shook my head. "I'm impressed."

When he stared at me coldly, I figured me telling him about the blackmailer and what Germaine did to me would make him talk.

"I have something important to talk to you about."

Before I could go any further, he pushed me back on the bed and vigorously removed my vintage, boyfriend jeans.

My aqua thongs didn't stand a chance either. They were ripped from my body. He was hungry for me and I loved it. Evidently, my message did the trick. I removed my black, Diesel scoop neck tank and flung it on the floor. All Kingston had to remove was the towel wrapped around his waist. It didn't take him long to dive in. There was no need for him to make me wet because that was taken care of as soon as I saw him.

"Oooooh......Kingston.....baby....I'm sorry," I apologized as he punished my pussy.

"Shut up!"

Yes, he was pissed and I loved it, especially when he lifted and pushed my legs above my head. I knew that I wasn't gonna be able to take the pounding he was about to lay on me. I tried to wriggle out of it, but to no avail.

"Ain't this what the fuck you wanted when you called my phone all fucking night?" he growled harshly.

"Baby! Baby! Baby, I.....I'm sorry," I pleaded.

His actions and words had me more than sure that my phone calls had gotten him in trouble with his wife. Moments later, he removed his dick, hopped off the bed, pulled me to the edge and forced me on all fours. I didn't have time to disagree before Kingston gripped my shoulders and pounded me from behind.

"Kingston! Kingston!"

He shoved my face into one of the pillows to muffle my cries. I managed to turn my head so that I could breathe, but he yanked my hair and shoved my face right back into the pillow. I wasn't into that asphyxiation shit, so I needed him to stop. I reached behind me and clawed at his thighs. I could tell that his ass was turned on because he began pounding me even harder. The more I fought to lift or turn my head, the more strength he seemed to gain. I grabbed the pillow and yanked it from under my face. I fought for air.

"Aaaaaaahhhhhhhh!" Kingston released as he unloaded inside of me. As soon as he did, he hopped up.

I collapsed while staring at him. "I'm not into that type of kinky shit, Kingston," I reprimanded once I caught my breath.

"That wasn't for your benefit."

I lay appalled while he disappeared into the bathroom. He was taking this jealousy and pissed off shit a little too far. Seconds later, I heard the shower running. I figured it was time to get something that benefited me. He'd deprived me of an orgasm so now he owed me. I walked to the door and turned the knob, but quickly realized that it was locked.

"This is fucking childish, Kingston!" I pouted.

I leaned against the door and folded my arms. Looking around the room, I spotted his shorts and shoes at the foot of the bed. I had to know more about him. I needed to know what I was getting myself into. It was my time to snoop.

Walking over, I removed his wallet from his shorts. Before I had a chance to get past the four hundred dollars and two credit cards, a slip of paper fell out. I picked it up and opened it. My mouth hit the floor when I saw my home address written on it. *What does he need my address for*? Better yet, what was he going to do with it?

"Anything interesting in there?" Kingston asked when he snuck up behind me.

I was so wrapped up in my mischief that I didn't realize the shower had stopped. As I listened, I realized that it was actually still running. I dropped the items on the floor then turned to him. He was wearing another towel around his waist while drying his glistening, bald head with another.

"I'm so sorry, Kingston," I quickly apologized.

"Whatever you saw in there, don't question me about any of it."

His facial expression told me that he meant business and I should agree to his demand.

"Okay," I answered obediently as I watched him pick up the wallet and paper from the floor and place them on the table. I guess he was confident that I wouldn't rummage through it again. I couldn't help myself. I needed to know. "Why do you have my address, Kingston?"

"What did I just tell you, Niquole?"

"But..."

"But nothing! Don't ask me any fucking questions!"

At that moment, Kingston approached me, wrapped the towel he was carrying around the back of my neck and pulled me to him. For the first time since I'd met him, I was afraid, but didn't know of what. I stared into his eyes.

"Are we on the same page?" He toyed with my hair then leaned down and pecked my lips. "Don't ask questions. Okay?"

"K...Kingston, I just..."

He gently jerked me closer to him with the towel. I could feel and smell his Doublemint breath. "I don't like repeating myself, Niquole."

My heart began to race and a lump formed in my throat. I was happy when I heard my phone ring. I needed that interruption. I ducked out of the towel and dashed to my purse. When I pulled the phone out, and saw Germaine's mother's number on the screen, a frown quickly displayed on my face. I knew I should've answered because my boys were probably with her, but I couldn't stomach that conversation right now.

"Turn it off," Kingston ordered.

"What?"

"You heard me. Turn it off."

"Kingston, I need to have my phone on. I have kids and I have a busy weekend ahead of me."

"I won't ask you again. Turn it off."

This definitely wasn't the Kingston I knew. He'd changed.

"Before I turn it off, I need to show you something." I waited for a reprimand, but surprisingly, he didn't give one. Pulling out some papers from my laptop bag, I walked over to him. "I'm in the process of meeting with a realtor to..."

"A realtor? For what?" He looked at the houses that I'd picked out for us to choose from and frowned.

Caught completely off guard, I replied, "For us. Me, you and my boys." I really didn't know what to think or how to feel when he burst out laughing.

"What possessed you to think that was something I wanted?" he asked after catching his breath. "Kids? Come on now."

My legs began to give out from under me. I had to sit down on the bed to keep from falling to the floor. If this was still part of his jealousy act, he was taking it too far.

"Do you know how much I love you, Kingston?" He didn't respond. I watched him redress as if I wasn't in the room. "What do I need to do to make this right?" Tears formed in my eyes as I poured my heart out to him. "If this has anything to do with Germaine being in the picture, you don't have to worry about him for long. I just need to make sure that he's not able to get my money; the money for you and me." My pleas weren't working so the tears that had formed in my eyes fell. "Kingston, talk to me! Stop ignoring me! I know you love me and I'm more than sure that you really don't wanna be with your wife. Besides, you killed for me and we're always together." It was time for him to prove his love for me yet again. "Germaine spit in my face and was about to slap me the other day because I wouldn't attend Hummer's funeral with him." Surprisingly, he chuckled.

"I told you that nigga was weak," Kingston responded and walked toward the door. "Order up some room service. I need to get something out of my truck." He walked out without waiting for me to agree or disagree.

I picked up one of my shoes off the floor and threw it at the door. He was really starting to piss me off. But I figured feeding him would lighten him up. I called room service and ordered two steaks, roasted potatoes, steamed shrimp and a bottle of champagne. After disconnecting the call, I heard a phone ring. I glanced at the night stand. He'd left his phone. I wondered if it was his wife calling. I walked over to the phone and my mouth dropped when I saw Meagan's name and number pop up.

"What the hell?" I fumed loudly. "They must've met at the album release party."

My mind raced a million miles per minute. What the fuck was she doing calling him? When did they have time to swap numbers? I had my eyes on him the entire night. I paced the room like a woman betrayed, but the betrayal was on him. Meagan had no way of knowing about my involvement with him. I tortured myself trying to figure out when they could've possibly found the time to connect. *When I was in the damn bathroom crying was the only time they could've met.* There was no way that her white ass was going to sink her claws into my man. *I'm sure she must've used some serious game for him to even get her number.* Meagan was cute, but her body certainly couldn't compare to mine. Besides, I already had to share him with his wife. I'd be damned if I shared him with *my* assistant. I made sure to keep a close eye on that bitch when I got back to Houston.

Suddenly, there was a knock at the door. I assumed Kingston must've left his key. I answered the door still in my birthday suit.

I gasped. "A.J.?"

"Damn, you already started without me?" he smiled while staring me up and down.

During all the chaos, I had forgotten all about him. He needed to leave. I didn't need Kingston any more pissed at me than he already was. A.J. stepped toward me and his lips went straight for my breasts. I stepped away. He walked inside and closed the door.

"Oh, you wanna play hard to get, huh? I remember when we used to play those games," he said before pulling me toward him.

I began secreting. I didn't know if those were the extra juices left behind from Kingston or freshly squeezed juices from being in A.J.'s presence.

"Ummmmm, A.J., as much as I would love to do this, I can't. You've got to get the hell out of here," I spoke frantically while shoving him back out the door.

"We haven't done that pretend rape thing in a while, but I'm down," he said while sexing me with his eyes. He stepped to me again. He needed to stop staring at me with those conniving, yet inviting gray eyes

"This is no joke, A.J. You have to leave."

"Why? You called me up here. What the hell is going on?"

"I know, but now is not a good time," I continued panicking.

A.J. looked me up and down again. He then walked around me as if I wasn't there and stood in front of the bed. It was completely tossed. Pillows were strewn on the floor and the covers were dangling from the bed. A.J. was no fool. I was sure he knew what had gone down.

"A.J., I'm begging you. Please leave."

"Someone beat me to the punch, huh?" he asked in a disappointed tone. "Did Germaine surprise you?"

"No. My man surprised me."

"Your man?"

"Yes, my man," I reiterated sassily.

"Still up to your old tricks, I see."

"No, this is different. I love him."

"That's fucked up, Niquole."

"How? You were coming up here to fuck me," I reminded. "You know what. It doesn't even matter. You need to leave. He went downstairs to get something and should be on his way back up," I said before pushing him out the door. However, A.J. managed to place his foot in the door before I closed it. "What, A.J? You're gonna get me in trouble."

"How in the hell can you get in trouble with a nigga that you're just fucking?" he asked like he was bothered by my words.

"He's not just any nigga. He's my man and will soon be replacing Germaine."

"Does he know this shit?" A.J. laughed.

I didn't have time for the lecture. He had to go. "Bye, A.J."

"Next time, don't call me. I'll call you."

He removed his foot as I finally closed the door. "Damn, that was a close call," I said, hoping like hell the two of them didn't pass each other in the hallway.

"Ma'am, we're landing in a few. I need to take your glass and I need for you to buckle up," the tall, well-endowed, stewardess smiled at me as she removed the wine glass from my flight tray.

I wanted to slap that smile off her face especially since she reminded me of Meagan's trifling ass. I yanked the seatbelt around my waist and buckled it as I thought about the phone call. I couldn't question either of them about it without someone becoming suspicious. Meagan would want to know if I was cheating on Germaine and Kingston would want to know if I snooped through his phone. As much as I didn't want to, I had to put that phone call in the back of my mind, but I knew it wouldn't stay there for long.

When the flight landed at George Bush International Airport, I hightailed off the plane like a woman on a mission. Besides the phone call, Kingston didn't make the weekend any better. I was sure he had some romantic and exciting things planned for us. Instead, all he did was lie up in the bed and rack up the pay-per-view and room service bill. We didn't even fuck again. The bad part about the whole weekend was that I'd missed scouting new talent for that bull shit.

"Shit!" I yelled loudly when I reached the baggage claim section. "I never turned my damn phone back on."

I pulled my Blackberry from my purse and powered it

back up. As soon as I did, it immediately started beeping informing me that I had loads of missed text and voice messages. Hitting #1 to activate my voicemail, the first message instantly disturbed me. It was from Germaine's mother informing me that he'd been in an accident the same day I arrived in New Orleans. I didn't bother to listen to the rest of the messages. Quickly, I grabbed my luggage when it came around the conveyor and raced out the terminal. Figuring I didn't want to waste time going to get my car, I decided to hail a cab instead.

"West Houston Medical Center on Richmond," I addressed the driver when I hopped inside.

While we drove, I contemplated calling my mother to see if she knew what was going on. I even thought about calling Germaine's mother. I decide not to bother either of them because I knew they were going to bite my head off.

When I arrived at the hospital several minutes later, I instantly rushed to the information desk. Seconds later, I was on the elevator headed to the second floor. There was no need to ask anyone what direction Germaine's room was in because as soon as I got off the elevator, I saw his entire cheering squad in the waiting room. It looked like they were having some type of meeting. Germaine's parents, my mom, Jalisa and Tyrell were all there. If looks could kill, I'd be dead. Germaine's mother gave me the most evil glare that I had ever seen. Tyrell even shook his head in disgust while Jalisa stood in her model stance with her arms folded shaking her head as well.

"What?" I snapped my neck at all of them. "I'm here, aren't I?"

"You're a sad ass excuse for a wife," Germaine's mother took a jab at me. "I wish my son had never met you."

"If your son hadn't met me, he wouldn't have shit," I jabbed back at her. If we weren't in a hospital, I probably would've stomped a mud hole in that bitch.

"Niquole, why did you turn your phone off?" my

mother chimed in to kill the tenseness. "You have kids. You can't be turning your phone off like that."

"Look, both of you can save this shit. I'm a grown ass woman. I don't have to answer to either one of you. I'm not Johnathan…you know the little boy who the two of you have more than me!"

"If you'd stay home and be a mother to them, then there would be no need for us to intervene," Germaine's mother blasted.

I stepped to her. "Look, Glenda…"

"This is neither the time nor the place," my mother said jumping between us.

"You know it's true," Glenda addressed my mother. "Your daughter is a sorry excuse for a wife and a mother. My son takes care of those boys…not her."

By my mother's facial expression, I was more than sure she was going to agree. I was just about to throw my phone directly at Glenda's head, when Tyrell hurried over to me. He stepped in my face like a lion about to demolish his prey.

"You need to watch yourself," he barked between gritted teeth before shoving my phone in my hand. "Go check on your fucking husband." He shoved me in the opposite direction. "Room 218."

I glared at them all before it hit me. Two people were missing.

"Where are my boys?" I asked.

"They're with my mom," Jalisa answered.

After receiving that confirmation, I slowly walked toward Germaine's room trying to think of something to say to him. Right before opening the door, I took a deep breath.

He looked at me then slowly turned away. He had a few visible scratches and bruises on his cheeks, arm and forehead. A sinister part of me wished his ass had been killed in the accident for spitting in my face.

I didn't want to be in that damn room. I wanted to be with my man who was now probably fucking Meagan. I looked at my phone then at Germaine. I couldn't resist. I dialed Meagan's number. It went straight to voicemail. I took a deep breath and blew it out hard. I had to shake the thought of the two of them rolling around in the sheets. I had to get a hold of myself.

"You can at least show some kind of damn compassion, Nikki," Germaine finally spoke. "I was damn near killed the other day and this is your first time seeing me since it happened. And you're over there on the fucking phone. You haven't even asked if I was okay."

"Well, are you?"

Before the dynamite could explode in the room, the door opened. Tyrell and another police officer walked inside. It didn't take long for Tyrell to shake his head at me again. He was probably pissed that I was standing by the door and not by Germaine's side. Little did he know, it didn't make any sense for me to pretend.

"Hey man," Tyrell's buff ass addressed Germaine. "I was just out there with your mom and pop. They say they're not leaving no matter how many times you kick them out your room."

Germaine laughed. I could tell that it hurt him to do so due to the horrific face he made.

"This is the first officer on the scene. Officer Brady," Tyrell introduced. "We just need to take down some information."

Germaine nodded.

"Any enemies that you know of? Anyone that may want to see you hurt?" Officer Brady got right to the point. I quickly wondered why he would ask such a question. I inched closer to them.

"Naw, man, why?"Germaine worried. "My brakes just went out on me."

"Your brakes didn't just go out, G. The line was cut," Tyrell informed him.

"You're lucky to be alive," the other officer joined in.

"The brake line was cut?" I questioned with a frightened look on my face.

All three of them turned to me.

"Yeah, the line was cut," Tyrell answered. "You know anything about that?" he asked inquisitively but with attitude like he felt or knew I had something to do with it.

"Now, why in the hell would I know something like that?" I blasted back.

Not wanting to be interrogated, I swung the room door open and rushed out. First the money, then the pictures, then my tires at the frat party and now this? After regrouping, Tyrell joined me in the hall. He stood in front of me with his arms folded.

"Anything you need to tell me?" he asked then stood in a drill sergeant stance.

"No. Why? Do you think I would?"

"Because you're acting kinda weird. It seems a little fishy that this happened when you were out of town."

Was he serious? Did he really think I was a suspect? I had to get him out of my face. "I'm acting weird, asshole, because I just found out that someone cut the brake line on Germaine's car."

"Don't act like you give a shit," he replied.

. "I'm not dignifying that with a response."

"You don't have to. Your actions always speak louder than your words."

This Johnny Bravo looking mofo was really testing me. "They do, huh?" I smiled. "Then tell me what this says." I said, just before walking off.

When Germaine returned home three days later, I didn't expect a swarm of folks to invade my home, but he wanted them there to welcome him back. I guess he figured the flowers, get well soon cards and phone calls weren't enough. I was in no mood for the circus. I had business to take care of regarding my label, but the slew of people in my house killed that idea. There was no way I was gonna get any work done with all the loud laughter and chatter going on. Germaine poured salt on the already festering wound of mine when he turned on the TV. I guess he figured the conversations and laughter in the house weren't loud enough.

Meagan had texted me earlier saying that she wasn't going to be able to make it to the shindig. I wondered how she even found out about it because I knew Germaine didn't invite her. It was a good thing she declined because I didn't want that bitch in my house anyway. I probably would've poisoned her food. As much as I tried, I couldn't shake that phone call out of my mind, but Germaine quickly helped me.

"Nikki, is there any Parmesan cheese here?" I leaned against the counter watching him open and close the cabinet doors. "One of my mom's friends just brought over some spaghetti."

"You're the one who cooks so you should know," I snapped.

"Guess you have a point there."

"Why did you invite all these people here, Germaine? You know I have things to do and you know I don't like people in my house touching my stuff."

"These people are my family and friends as well as yours. They were worried about me," Germaine replied after turning to face me.

"You could've just picked up the damn phone and called them or better yet, you could've gone to see them."

"Not today, Nikki."

"Niquole!" I corrected.

"Whatever, Niquole," he replied before burying his face inside the refrigerator.

"What are you doing?" I asked when I saw him retrieve a bottle of Moscato from the refrigerator.

"It's for the guests."

"No, that's mine," I said after walking over and snatching the bottle from his hand. "If they want alcohol, they need to go buy some."

"You're a piece of work," Germaine boiled before slamming the refrigerator door then walking away to rejoin the circus.

I wasn't in the mood to be around anyone so I took my bottle of wine and walked out the back door. I plopped down on one of the lounge chairs by the pool, removed the wine stopper from the bottle then turned it up.

"Who is he, Niquole?"

I almost spit the wine out. I looked up at my mother who was sporting a nice, long jet black, wig.

"This has nothing to do with a man, Mama," I lied before taking another swig from the bottle.

"You can lie to anyone else, but you sure as hell can't lie to me. I know you. So, who is he?"

"None of your business. Leave it alone."

"Nikki, don't do this again."

"Mama, will you leave me alone. You don't know what you're talking about."

"Yes, I do. This situation has Mr. Hughes and that record exec, A.J. Townes written all over it."

I was furious that she'd brought that shit up. "Go ahead! Tell me how much of a bitch I am!"

"You said it. I didn't. Germaine doesn't deserve this, Nikki. He's a good man. If you don't want him then leave."

"I'm trying." Her facial expression told me that for once, she was shocked. "The only difference now is that I have money to look after."

"What about the boys?" she asked like I'd forgot them.

"You already know that's a definite. Wherever I go, they go."

"This isn't right and you know it. Your track record is terrible. You always gotta have what you want no matter who gets hurt in the process. Your daughter will never know her mother or her father."

My eyes bulged. "Why in the hell are you bringing this shit up, Mama? See, this is the reason why we don't get along. You're always in my damn business! You're always telling me how to run my life!"

"You need to let go of your evil and selfish ways."

"Well, I would've never had the baby if A.J. hadn't lied and told me that we would be together and the same goes for Mr. Hughes."

"Did you really think they were gonna leave their wives for you?"

"Yes," I answered boldly. "They told me they loved me."

"They're men, Nikki. They say whatever to get what they want."

"Well, why can't that shit work for me? Why can't I get what the fuck I want?" I questioned.

"Why couldn't you be like your sister? You've always

been trouble."

I winced at the thought of her bringing up my sister Adrienne who was five years older than me. She and I had different fathers. When I was ten, her dad convinced my mother to let Adrienne move with him to Chicago. She agreed. I barely knew my sister and neither did my mother for that matter, so it pissed me off when she compared me to her.

"How can you compare me to someone that you barely fucking know?" I lashed at her. "She got a better deal than I did anyway. She moved out of your house!"

"I do know her," she defended. "I know that she's a good person. She agreed to take your child, didn't she?"

At this point, I was fuming.

"I didn't want the kid. Adrienne couldn't have any so she agreed to take the baby and raise her as her daughter so it all worked out perfectly," I blasted. "Besides, she gets a hefty child support check each month from A.J. and me as well. She ain't complaining so why the hell should I? Why the hell should you for that matter? Why the hell should I fuck up the home that the child knows?"

My mother shook her head as I continued.

"And as far as Cierra goes, she thinks she's my niece so to hell with that."

"I think you're in over your head. You didn't win Mr. Hughes by sleeping with him and you didn't win A.J. or that major advertising he promised toward your record by sleeping with him either."

"You're right, but I did get something out of it. That bastard gave me the money to start my own label to keep the baby and our affair a secret. So, I came out on top."

"I wish you had aborted Cierra because she doesn't deserve you as a mother."

"I'm not her fucking mother! It was too late for me to abort her just like it was too late for me to abort Johnathan and Nathan."

"Oh my God!" she gasped. "You're so damn evil."

"Don't act like this is a shock to you. I love my boys, but I didn't want them at the time.'

"What about Cierra? Do you love her?"

I stared into my mother's eyes and answered, "As my niece...yes."

"She needs to know her cousins are really her brothers."

"No, she doesn't!"

"What are you gonna tell Germaine if he ever finds out?"

I glared at her. "He won't. That happened a year before I even met him and frankly, it's none of his fucking business."

"Nikki…"

"Damn, Mama! Will you please leave this shit alone?"

She didn't listen. "Has this new guy told you that he loves you?" I cut my eyes at her and clenched my teeth together. "He hasn't has he?"

"He doesn't have to. I know he loves me. He shows me everyday," I replied with my head held high.

"Nikki, you need to get some help. There…"

I jumped up from the chair and stormed back inside the house. I didn't need to hear that shit. I knew what I did and I was tired of hearing her bring it up. I knew Kingston loved me and she or no one else was going to make me think otherwise. My mother on my ass and the chitter and chatter in the house had worked my nerves. I walked into the living room and shocked everyone.

"Get the hell out of my house!"

"What in the hell is wrong with you?" Germaine barked then jumped in my face.

"They need to leave. I need to work."

"Take your ass to the studio and work. You're always running there anyway."

He had lost his mind. I walked around him like he was

nothing and stood firm before everyone. "Get out!"

No one waited for Germaine to put his foot down. They whispered and snickered, but I didn't care as long as they did it on their way out the door.

"That was fucking uncalled for! Do you know how embarrassing that was?" Germaine addressed me.

"Uhm, I'm gonna take the boys back to the house with me," my mother intervened before Germaine and I went to blows.

"There's no need, Ms. Wright," Germaine addressed her.

"Go ahead, Mama. Take them with you."

Germaine frowned at me. I knew he was tired of me defying him, but hell, the kids didn't need to be there. The argument wasn't over and deep down, he knew this as well. My mother knew what was best and took the boys.

"Niquole, you need to cool it," Jalisa added. "Don't act this way in front of your kids." By that time, my boys were already out the door. "Why are you acting like this? This is unnecessary. These people are your family and friends. They're here to support your husband."

Like I really needed to hear that last line. She said that shit on purpose to see my reaction. I had one for her though. "Jalisa, get out of my face. When I kicked everyone out of my house that included you as well."

She shook her head at me then turned to Germaine who was huffing and puffing like a raging bull. "Germaine, maybe we should just leave," she addressed him. "You need to cool off and I think I need to do the same before I say some shit that Nikki won't like."

Is this bitch really trying me? "Yeah, you really need to leave now," I threatened her. "Germaine, you may wanna take her advice."

It was more than obvious that he wanted to rip me a new asshole and Jalisa must've sensed that as well. She grabbed his arm and led him out the door rubbing his back in the process.

Around one a.m. my cell phone rang. I was still awake TiVo-ing missed episodes of *The Real L Word* on Showtime. Even though it was a gay show, I loved the catty drama. Looking at the phone, I quickly pressed the ignore button. Seconds later, it rang again.

"What, Germaine?" I answered furiously.

"Can you come out in the garage?"

I could tell in his voice that he was hammered…again. "For what?"

"Can you just do this one thing for me?" he whined.

I listened to the garage door open and pressed the pause button on the remote. "I'm coming," I huffed before hanging up. When I reached the garage, he was leaning against his truck finishing off a Heineken. "What do you want?"

"You."

"I don't have time for this silly shit, Germaine," I said before turning to walk back inside the house. He raced to the door and stopped me. "Move!" I demanded.

"You haven't let me touch you in almost a year." He used his body to back me against his truck.

"Germaine, move!"

"Please. I haven't touched or smelled you in so long."

I started to feel a little bit uncomfortable when he slid the spaghetti strap of my satin gown off my shoulder. I quickly pulled it back up. I assumed this angered him because he forced his tongue inside my mouth. The taste of beer and cigarettes made me gag. I shoved him. That angered him even more. At that moment, he pinned me against the truck with his body and kicked my legs open with his knees.

"What in the hell are you doing?"

"Don't deny me this, Nikki," he breathed freakishly in my ear. "Do not deny me this. You owe me."

I tried to shove him again, but he grabbed my hands and forced them above my head. I tried to wiggle away from him, but couldn't. His weight against me was more than I could handle. When he slipped his fingers inside my panties, all I could see was Hummer's face. Germaine was violating me in the same way. I leaned toward his ear and bit it as hard as I could then kneed him in his groin. Before cupping over in pain, the son-of-a-bitch punched me like I was a dude off the street. I was on my way to the pavement, before he caught me by the neck. I could see the anger, hurt, pain and frustration in his eyes as he choked me until I passed out.

Chapter Seventeen

For two days, I posted back up at the Hyatt Regency after the altercation between me and Germaine. I still couldn't believe that he'd punched and choked me until I passed out. When I regained consciousness, he was gone. It didn't take long for me to decide that I wasn't going to be there when he got back, so I left. He blew my phone up with apologies after apologies, but I wasn't trying to hear any of them. Meagan was blowing my phone up as well. As much as I didn't want to talk to her, I had no other choice. I was very blunt and standoffish when I told her that I'd be away for a few days and when she questioned what was wrong, I gladly told her none of her fucking business.

After learning that I'd be gone, she reminded me of calls that I had to make and messages that I needed to respond to. I nearly blew an internal head gasket when she asked if I wanted her to handle any of them. She was probably handling more than that with Kingston. With as much anger and disgust I could conjure up, I told her no and hung up in her face. That anger was due to all the images that had popped up in my head of her wallowing around with my man. Even all the calls that Jalisa made to me were answered by my voicemail. I damn sure didn't want to talk to her.

On my third day in the hotel, I called and told my mother to bring the boys so they could spend the night with me. Of course she wanted to know what was going on, but I didn't tell her anything. It was none of her business as well. I didn't need to give her any more ammunition to use against me and throw up in my face whenever she felt the need to. It was a different story when she made it to the hotel.

"So, do you plan on living like this for the rest of your life?" she asked then peeped through my luggage. I ignored her as I snatched Nathan out of her arms and playfully tossed him in the air. Johnathan had grabbed hold of my leg and the three of us fell back onto the bed after I lost my balance. "I know you hear me talking to you, Nikki."

I took a deep breath before replying, "Mama, you can leave now. Thank you for dropping the boys off." I gave her a stern look to let her know that I was serious about her leaving.

"I talked to your sister yesterday," she egged on as if I hadn't spoken a word.

"And?"

"She's flying down next month. It would be nice if the boys saw their…"

"She's not their damn sister. How many times must I tell you that?" My mother knew that she was pissing me off. Part of me wondered if that was her intention.

"Cierra came from you. She's your daughter. How in the hell can you not see that when you carried her for nine months?"

I ignored that question. "Can you leave now so that I can have some time alone with my *boys*?"

"Time alone?" She turned toward the television. "Looks to me like you're already geared up to have the TV take care of them." She was referring to the children's show line up that was scrolling up the screen. "Time alone is you actually tending to them and not the damn TV."

I laid Nathan on the bed next to Johnathan who had his face buried in the soft, down comforter. I stood up and got in my mother's face. "Just because you didn't raise me right doesn't mean that I'm gonna be the same way toward my boys."

"What do you mean by not raising you right?" she asked as if I'd insulted her. "You didn't give me a chance to."

It was time for me to tell her why I hated her so much. "You still don't know why I left after I graduated high school, do you?"

"I figured you left because of the continued backlash you got from fucking around with that teacher and getting him fired," she sassed.

"Believe me, that had nothing to do with it." That smug look on her face slowly disappeared. "I was always pissed at you for kicking my father out of the house."

"There were some things you wouldn't have understood," she countered.

"What about now? Would I understand them now?"

"It really doesn't matter now, Nikki."

"Well, let me finish. Besides being pissed at you for getting rid of my father, I had other reasons. I read your diary when I was sixteen."

"What does my diary have to do with any of this, Nikki?" she asked trying to force down that lump that had formed in her throat.

"On page twenty-three, you prayed to God that I never had any kids because I was a selfish and devilish bitch."

"Well, you are and you know it."

It was time to let her have it. I knew why she felt that way about me. "You're still pissed that your boyfriends wanted me and not you." I expected a few harsh words after my statement, but I didn't expect the slap.

"I could never keep a man because of your whorish ass!" she yelled.

I held onto my face. "You had a man, but you kicked him out!"

"You're an evil lil' bitch. Is there anyone on this earth

that you give a damn about?"

I glanced down at my boys. "I give a damn about them."

"You don't give a damn about these boys. You don't deserve them."

I laughed. "Please enlighten me as to how I don't give a damn."

"You're never around. Germane is their mom and dad."

"Yeah. Yeah, Whatever."

"I was happy when you left my house," she continued.

"Why because you knew the threat was gone," I replied. "Don't be pissed at me because you didn't know how to please a man. Besides, you let it go on for as long as you did. You kept bringing those men around me and I kept giving them what they wanted, to get what *I wanted.*"

She was flabbergasted and her face told that story. "You're crazy," my mother said in a frightened voice. "All of this for a damn man? Nikki, you can't make men love you! You can't blackmail men into loving you!" she yelled as if her heightened voice would rattle some sense into me.

"I guess you realized that after *your* numerous failed attempts, huh?"

She tried to slap me again, but this time I caught her hand before it landed. "I'm no longer that teenager who sat back and took these slaps from you." There was a ten second stare down before I released her arm. "Get out of my fucking room," I growled at her.

Staring at me one final time, she kissed the boys before walking toward the door.

"Germaine doesn't deserve this, Nikki. Maybe the others did, but he doesn't."

"All I want from him is to let me out of this marriage with my money and my boys so that I can go be with my man."

"Those boys deserve and need stability, Nikki. You're

too wrapped up in yourself to give them that."

After that last statement, she walked out.

On day four, I dropped the boys off at daycare, then met with the realtor who helped me with the purchase of my home. It was time to get this plan in motion. I felt that I needed to do a whole lot of convincing to show and prove to Kingston that I was serious.

"Hi, Niquole. It's nice to see you again," the chubby, gray haired realtor greeted me with a huge smile and handshake from across his desk.

"Same here, Henry."

I shook his hairy hand and sat down in one of the padded chairs.

"So, you're ready to do this?" he smiled hard showing his bright, white veneers. He was set to profit a huge chunk of change from the $575,000 dollar home if he sold it.

"I think so, Henry. I still need to fly out to Sarasota to actually see the house. The virtual tour is great, but it's nothing like the real thing."

"You're right and I don't blame you, but let me tell you this. There are a few more offers on the house and I don't think it's going to wait for you."

"Now, let me ask you this." I put my game face on and leaned closer toward his desk. "Does money still talk?"

"It sure does in my world."

"Well, make it happen," I said before standing up and sliding my green, Balenciaga bag over my shoulder.

"So, did Germaine like the virtual tour of the house?" Henry asked with dollar signs in his eyes.

My body tensed at the mention of his name. I turned to him and smiled. "It's a surprise, so don't mention it."

"Gotcha," Henry responded.

As I walked out the door, my phone rang. It was my mother. "What do you want?" I asked after answering.

"Germaine wanted me to call and tell you that he has the boys and you need to call him."

Before I could respond, she disconnected the call. I hesitated before dialing his number.

"I just dropped them off. Why did you go pick them up?" I immediately chewed him out when he answered.

"The daycare called and told me that Johnathan was sick."

"Sick?" I questioned. "He wasn't sick when I dropped him off. Why didn't they call me?"

"Because they knew which one of us would pick him up," he answered. "You need to come home."

When those words slithered through my ear, all I could think about was him being dead. I pressed the end button on my phone to avoid hearing him begging me to come home or his pathetic apologies. I needed to remain pissed at him to focus on how he was gonna end up paying for his actions. He could've killed me and didn't even know it since his bitch ass left me passed out on the garage floor. That was probably what he had wanted anyway. *Damn, I wish he would've died in that car accident*. I wish I knew who fucked with his brakes so they could attempt it again. Whatever the price, I was willing to pay.

Kingston needed to know what he did to me. He didn't seem too pissed about Germaine spitting in my face so maybe the news of him punching me then choking me nearly to death would make his blood boil. I needed him pissed off like he was when Hummer tried to rape me. In other words, I wanted him to off Germaine. I pressed the number two button on my phone. Kingston answered on the first ring.

"Yeah," he said as if I had disturbed him.

I forced up a few tears and altered my voice as if I'd

been crying. "Baby, Germaine tried to kill me." There was no need to sugarcoat the situation.

"Can this wait?"

I instantly fumed. "What? No!" I screamed into the phone. I was pissed off at the fact that my words didn't stir him. "You need to handle him, Kingston like you did Hummer!"

"You need to watch what the fuck you say over these damn phones," he chastised. "I'll deal with you later."

I looked at my phone to see if the call was still active. It wasn't. He had hung up. What was I doing wrong? What had I done wrong? Why had he changed all of a sudden? Something else had to be going on with him. I needed to find out.

Chapter Eighteen

After five unsuccessful attempts to reach Kingston once he hung up on me, he turned off his phone. My last attempt went straight to voicemail. I figured he must've been with his wife, but he still needed to talk to me. If we were gonna do this couple thing, we needed to get our shit together and get rid of the excess baggage. We needed to move on with our lives.

As much as I didn't want to, I decided to go back to the house just in case Johnathan was actually sick. When I arrived, I slowly walked inside and found Germaine sitting on the sofa. He was drinking a beer as usual and smoking a cigarette. I wanted to curse him out for doing so but, I didn't feel like arguing with him.

"Where's Johnathan?" I asked after scouring the living room.

When he saw me, he put the cigarette out and finished off his Heineken. "He's still at daycare," he answered after standing up.

"What the hell, Germaine? Why did you lie?"

"Because I knew that was the only way to get you here."

"That's fucked up. I can't believe you used your damn son and then you have my mother in on this shit, too."

"I needed you to come home."

"I don't have time for your meaningless apologies." I turned to walk out the door, but he stopped me by tossing a manila envelope at my feet. I stared at it for a few seconds hoping and praying that it contained divorce papers. I knelt down and picked it up. "What's this?"

"That night after the album release party, I saw you go outside to the trash." It felt like my throat was closing because I could hardly breathe. My body tensed up. I knew what he was about to say next. "I got the jacket, Nikki."

I had to think of something quick. "Your nasty ass dug through the trash for something that…"

"Save it, Nikki," Germaine cut me off. I was puzzled when he picked up an Omega Psi Phi frat pin from off the table. "This was in your jacket pocket."

"And?" I wondered how it got there.

"It's not mine, Nikki. Where did you get it from?"

My throat closed even tighter when it dawned on me that Kingston must've slipped the pin inside my pocket. But why? Was he trying to make me take the fall for the murder? I shook that thought quickly. I was supposed to get rid of the jacket so the pin would've been gone, too. So, blackmailing me was out of the question.

"Is it Hummer's pin?" Germaine asked pulling me away from my thoughts.

"What? Why in the hell would I have that asshole's pin?"

"Nikki…"

"Niquole!" I corrected.

"It really doesn't matter at this fucking point, Nikki…Niquole. What do you think is in that envelope?"

I stared at the envelope then back at him. "I hope divorce papers."

He laughed. "You would hope that wouldn't you?"

I became a little concerned after realizing that I was wrong. "What is it then?"

"I had that blood on your jacket tested. You hold the results of the test in your hand."

My fingers became putty and the envelope slipped out of my hand. "Why did you do that? Better yet, how in the hell did you do it?"

"Tyrell is a cop and I have a few frat brothers that work in labs so, it wasn't hard," Germaine said with a smug look on his face.

I tormented myself for a little over a minute as I tried to picture my body draped in prison attire. What the hell had I gotten myself into? It was my fault that Germaine found everything because I didn't do what Kingston had told me. Now, because of my brutal mistake, he and I may be going to jail.

"I'm waiting," Germaine ripped through my thoughts again. I watched him fold his arms across his chest. "Ni..."

"Hummer is a son-of-a-bitch and he deserved to die for what he tried to do to me!" I blasted leaving him speechless and stunned.

His arms fell to his sides in disbelief. His actions were not of a person who already knew the answer to his own question. I glanced down at the envelope on the floor. I picked it up with the quickness and ripped it open. I furiously flipped through the stack looking for answers. None. Blank sheets of paper were all I saw. I turned back to Germaine.

"You played me!" I yelled, then threw the papers in his face.

"You played your-fucking-self," he replied in a tone and with a look like he didn't know who the hell I was. "You had something to do with Hummer getting killed?"

I could no longer stand the heat. "I'm outta here," I said before making a turn toward the door. When I opened it, Germaine immediately slammed it shut. I couldn't face him.

"Who killed my friend, Nikki, because I know you didn't do it?" he asked before placing his hand under my chin. He forced me to look at him. “Who did you pay to kill Hummer?”

I watched his skin change colors and those eyebrows connect. He was furious and I needed to get the hell out of dodge. I couldn’t answer him without having to give up Kingston, and I wasn’t prepared to do that. I stood silent.

“So, you’re just gonna stand there and say nothing?”

I couldn’t keep quiet any longer. There was one thing that I needed to know. “Are you gonna turn me in?”

Germaine stepped away from me as if I was diseased. He then gave me one last pissed off yet disgusted look from head to toe then walked out of the house. I was happy he did because I was seconds away from passing out.

I paced my office for nearly two hours wondering what disturbing ideas were brewing inside of Germaine’s head. I couldn’t go to Kingston with the information because I’d told him that the jacket was taken care of. I had to swing the ball back into my court. I knew what I had to do.

Around one a.m., I heard Germaine trip inside the house. I knew he’d be drunk when he returned and I knew he’d be stunned when he saw the house filled with candles. He didn’t see me at the top of the stairs. I pressed the play button on the stereo remote and the first CD in rotation began. R. Kelly sifted from the Bose speakers and throughout the house. I needed the ambiance to be on point.

“Nikki! What in the hell is all of this?” he spoke loudly.

I walked back to his bedroom and slammed the door as hard as I could making sure it was loud enough for him to hear. It worked. Seconds later, he opened the door.

“W…What’s all this?” Germaine stuttered when he saw me lying on his bed in Agent Provocateur lingerie. I could tell that he was really drunk, but I was going to have to look past that.

"Like you told me before, you haven't touched me in almost a year so, I thought we could spend the night touching each other," I said seductively.

"Oh really?" he questioned then stumbled over to the bed.

I cringed when I felt his hand start from my foot and trace its way up to my thong. I hated feeling his hands on me, but I had to do what I had to do. Seconds after feeling all over my body, he ripped through the babydoll dress like a hungry animal. He wanted me…bad. That was good, but I needed to regain control before he demolished me. I rose up on my knees and pushed him backward.

I smiled at him."Me first." If only he knew how painful it was to make that simple expression.

He anxiously kicked off his Nikes as I unbuckled his belt then his jeans. I seductively removed them as well as his Calvin Klein boxers.

"It has been a long time, hasn't it, baby?" he slurred.

"Yes, it has. Long overdue." I winced at my words.

I had to catch myself from gagging. I didn't want to do what I was about to do, but I had no other choice. I'd be damned if I was going to spend the next twenty-five years to life in prison scrubs. I took a deep breath before bowing my head to his. As soon as I breathed on his dick, it rose to the nine inches that I remembered. I had to give myself a pep talk. I closed my eyes and pretended that he was Kingston. As soon as I latched onto him, he immediately began moaning.

"Damn, Niquole! Baby, I miss this."

At that moment, I didn't want him to call me Niquole. I wanted to be Nikki to him again. My head dipped and bobbed at a nice pace as my saliva trickled down his dick. Seconds later, the son-of-a-bitch began rolling around in my mouth then ran his fingers through my hair. I teased the tip with my tongue and he nearly lost it.

"You like that, baby?" I asked when I came up for air five minutes later.

"Yeah. Don't stop," Germaine ordered as he helped my head back down.

Okay, damn it! I'm not about to be down here for another five minutes. I should've rethought my strategy because I knew it was going to be hard for him to cum since he was drunk. I bobbed, dipped and stroked for what seemed like forever.

"Mmmmm, baby, I need you inside of me," I whined then climbed on top of him. "I need to see what I've been missing."

This shit was really killing me, but I had to make sure that I put on a damn good show. So far so good. Germaine surprised me when he stuck two of his fingers inside my pussy. I was even getting a little pissed off at myself because I was beginning to enjoy it. That wasn't part of the plan. I found myself riding his fingers.

"You like that, Nikki?" he asked. "You want this dick on that pussy, baby?"

"Ooooooh…yes!" I wanted to slap myself.

"We can do that," he agreed, "but not like you think we're gonna do it."

Suddenly, he stopped. I was confused as I watched Germaine lean over to his nightstand and pull out a few condoms from the drawer. What in the hell were those doing in there? All I could think about was him having a bitch in my house when I wasn't home. He handed me one of the condoms.

"What is this for?" I asked staring at the Trojan.

"*We* haven't fucked in nearly a year, but I'm more than sure that *you* have," he stressed.

"Why do you have rubbers in here, Germaine?" I asked curiously.

"Do you really think I'm going inside of you bare?" I

was stunned by his words, but he was right. I couldn't blame him. "I had them in case something eventually popped off between me and you. I wanted to be prepared."

I gave him a crazy look.

"Put it on me," he ordered. I stared at him for a brief moment. "What are you waiting for Niquole..Nikki or whoever the hell you wanna be called? This is what you wanted, right?" Although he was drunk, he was very alert. I didn't want him to be that way. I ripped the wrapper open then rolled the condom onto him. "Now what?" he asked as he stared back at me.

Going through with the plan, I lifted myself up and attempted to maneuver my pussy over the tip of his dick to get it back wet, but he had other ideas. He gripped my hips and pushed me down on him. I screamed since I was still a little dry. "This is what you wanted, right?" Germaine asked as he forcefully helped me ride him. His nails dug deep into my thighs. "Act like you want it, Nikki," he demanded as he thrust harder and deeper inside of me. "Pretend I'm him."

I wanted to cry, but fought the urge.

"Ooooooh…Germaine…" I played out my part.

"You must really think I'm fucking stupid, huh?" he asked causing me to halt the ride. But he made me pick the pace back up. "Don't think this changes shit. I still wanna know who killed my fucking friend. Now, continue fucking me. I've got all night." My plans had taken an immediate nosedive. He'd been onto me all along. "You can do better than that, can't you?" Germaine asked sarcastically as I rode him with no enthusiasm. "You need some help?" I could feel the tears in the back of my eyes, but I kept them at bay. I didn't want to give him that satisfaction. Instead, I lifted my body up a little and planted my feet on the mattress. "That's what I'm talking 'bout, baby," he jeered. "Just like old times. Talk to me, baby." He had to be joking. How much more torture was he expecting me to endure? "Talk!" he barked.

"This feels so good, baby," I moaned.

"Ride it! Ride it" he demanded then tried to match my rhythm. I couldn't take it anymore. I wanted to get off this train. It was pointless to me now. I stopped and tried to climb off of him, but he grabbed me. "What in the hell are you doing?" Germaine asked like he was dumbfounded by my move.

I shook my head. "I'm not doing this with you anymore, Germaine."

"So, you thought you were gonna try and play me? You thought that by fucking me I would forget what I know? You wanna know my intentions? You wanna know what I plan on doing with the evidence?"

I slowly nodded my head and said, "Yes."

"So, now the ball is in my corner, huh?"

When I nodded again, Germaine slid from under me and onto his knees. He caressed my face and stared into my eyes then whispered, "You will never know. Now, let's finish what you started."

I was now on my back taking him, listening to him groan in my ear and feeling him squeezing my breasts. All I could do was lie there and let him have his way with me. Now, I really wanted him dead.

Around ten the next morning, I woke up and rolled over onto a used condom. At that moment, Germaine's seeds gushed out of it and onto my stomach. Disgusted, I grabbed the beige sheet and wiped it off. He even had the nerve to have his hand on my thigh. He didn't move when I pushed that shit off me. He wouldn't have known the difference anyway because his ass was passed out. Pulling my naked body up, I sat at the foot of the bed and shook my head at the used condoms on the floor. Even my lingerie had been practically ripped to shreds.

He had a field day with me and I can't do a damn thing about it, I thought.

My entire body was soar. I wanted to grab one of the pillows and smother his ass with it. I actually would've done it if I didn't think he would wake up. As Germaine went into second gear with his loud snores, I took one last glance at him. I wished I had a butcher knife. I definitely would've Lorena Bobbitted his ass while he slept.

Disregarding that thought, I slowly opened the door and slithered out then rushed to the bathroom to take a shower. While I let the water attempt to soothe my body, I allowed thoughts from that night before to swarm my mind. I wanted to vomit when Germaine kissed me and filled my mouth with his alcohol ridden breath. When he was on top of me, the alcohol seeped through his pours and dripped onto my skin and into my eyes causing them to burn. The only thing I could do was lay there and take whatever he dished at me. I was pissed, and determined to get him back at all cost.

After showering, I glanced in Germaine's room and quickly realized that he was still asleep. Trotting to my office, I went straight to my laptop that was still on. It also had the words, incorrect password highlighted on the screen.

"That son-of-a-bitch must've been snooping when I finally fell asleep," I mumbled to myself.

I couldn't help but laugh at his sad tactics. Not unless he knew Kingston on a first name bases, he would never figure out my password.

I sat down in my chair, threw my head back and took a deep breath as thoughts of the past few months skipped through my brain. How in the hell had I gotten myself in such deep shit? The only way for me to get out of it was to tell Kingston, but that was going to be hard. Not only would he be pissed, but I'm sure he would never trust me again. I couldn't have that. One thing was for sure though, I needed to get out of that house with Germaine before he woke up. I don't think I could take another sex session with him. My body now belonged to Kingston and Germaine had violated it.

I pushed myself up out of the chair and hurried to my closet. I pulled a pair of dark Seven jeans followed by a black embellished tank top, and some Giuseppe ballerina flats. I didn't have time to dress to impress right now. After placing my hair behind my ears, I grabbed my laptop. I didn't wanna leave it behind for fear that Germaine would destroy it or better yet, find a way to get inside. I was just about to close down the screen then thought about checking my emails really quick. As soon as I opened my account, my heart rate increased.

$50,000 by tomorrow or your hubby gets the pics of you and your lover.

I glanced over the email a few times before pressing

the reply button. I knew I wouldn't get a response just like all the other times I'd sent one, but whoever it was had to know that I was serious. I'd had enough of this bullshit.

Do whatever-the-fuck you wanna do because I ain't paying you another fuckin' dime.

I'd given up over $80,000 since this shit first started, so the game was about to end here. *If Germaine finds out what's going on, fuck it. I'll just see his ass in court.*

I closed the laptop, grabbed my brown Bottega Veneta hobo bag off my desk and flew out of the house. My first thought after hopping in my car were my boys. I needed to get them and the person that was going to help me was my mother. The bitch owed me anyway.

Twenty minutes after leaving the house, I swerved into my mother's yard, jumped out of my car and hurried to her front door. She'd changed the locks a few months back and still hadn't bother to give me a key, so I had to knock like a fucking stranger. I didn't bother to ask why either because I already knew. She didn't want me in her house unless she was there. Her ass probably thought I would brush up on her man. Sadly, she was probably right.

I rang the doorbell and knocked on the door like a mad woman. Eventually, she yanked it open. I could tell she was pissed. After staring her up and down, I watched her tie her baby blue satin robe then run her fingers through her hair.

"Were you fucking?" I asked.

"What in the hell do you want, Nikki?" she answered in an extremely irritated tone then closed the door behind her.

"I need your help." When she folded her arms across her chest, I frowned. "I'm sorry. Did I say something wrong?" I questioned after watching the attitude form on her face.

"Why in the hell would I help you with anything?"

"Bitch, because you owe me!"

"Owe you? Owe you?" my mother asked as if she couldn't believe her ears. "I don't owe you anything. I…"

"Let me stop you right there. I think I came at you wrong."

"Yes, you did," she agreed.

"Well, let me fix that. You're *gonna* help me."

She smiled sinisterly "Again, why should I help you?"

I guess my mother thought she had me by the reigns, but she must've forgotten who I was.

"It won't take much for me to revert back to that teenager who used to take all your men. I'm sure that I've been the topic of several conversations between you and your beau." Her smile quickly diminished and she unfolded her arms. I had her.

"What do you want, Niquole?" she asked in a defeated tone.

"I need you to go pack some things. I need you and the boys to hide out for a while."

Her eyebrows crinkled "Hide out? What? What's going on?"

"Look, I've got some things I need to figure out. You need to…"

"What do the boys have to do with this?" she interrupted.

"Just go pack a bag. I'll be in the car waiting. Hurry up because I've gotta get the boys."

I didn't wait for a reply. Instead, I walked to my car, sat inside and waited. After ten minutes, I began honking my horn. She needed to hurry up.

Seconds after blowing my horn a few more times, her lover appeared in the door. She was right behind him with a duffel bag. After kissing him on the lips, she finally headed toward my car. He waved at me, but I rolled my eyes at the six-feet-three, chocolate God. I couldn't stand that bastard since he turned me down when I made a pass at him weeks before I met Kingston. I wondered if things would be different since I was no longer pregnant. It didn't matter, I had a man now.

"So, where are we going?" my mother asked when she slid her seatbelt on.

"Germaine's mom's house."

A petrified look formed on her face after those words, but she said nothing. I guess she knew that we were about to drive through the gates of hell. The twenty-five minute drive to Germaine's mom's house was quiet. Obviously, neither of us wanted to push the other's buttons.

"I'll be right back," I addressed to her when I pulled into Germaine's mother's driveway.

"Don't do anything crazy, Nikki," she said to me before I stepped out the car.

"As long as that bitch doesn't…I'm cool."

I took long, hard steps toward the house like a landlord about to evict a tenant. After climbing the three steps, I rang the doorbell. Instantly, I heard Johnathan yelling to his grandmother that someone was at the door. Moments later, she opened it. You would've thought that I was the grim reaper from her expression.

"May I help you?" Glenda asked as if I had no business coming to her house.

I returned the same evil glare she was giving me. "I'm picking up my boys."

"Germaine didn't run that by me."

I jerked my head back in disbelief then lit into her ass. "Germaine doesn't have to run shit by you when it comes to my kids."

"Well…"

"Well, nothing!" I pushed her out the way and stormed inside the house to collect my children.

"You need to get the hell out of my house!" Glenda

walked up behind me as I lifed Nathan from his playpen. "You can't take them. I have to call Germaine."

"Call him!" I screamed, startling Nathan in the process.

"What's going on in here?" Germaine's passive father limped from the back of the house like we'd just disturbed his sleep.

"She's trying to take the boys," Glenda informed him.

He turned to me. "Niquole, what's going on? Did you and my son have a fight or something?"

If only he knew. "I just came to get my boys."

"Let's just call Germaine," he said thinking that would satisfy the situation.

"Like I told your wife, I don't have to get permission to get my children," I addressed him. "But if you want to feel like you did something, go ahead and call him. Good luck getting his drunk ass on the fucking phone!"

"Drunk?" Glenda asked in shock. "My son doesn't drink."

I laughed. "You've got to be fucking kidding me. All your son does is sit, drink and smoke all day." I watched as she grab the black cordless phone from the coffee table. I assumed she was calling Germaine and as I expected, he didn't answer. "You can call the house or his cell all you want," I said when Glenda started dialing again. "You might stand a better chance by just dropping by the house."

"You are a wicked lil' tramp," she growled at me. "If he is drinking, I'm sure it's because of you!"

"Oh well. Wouldn't be the first time a man did something crazy because of me," I smiled wickedly as I thought back to Kingston killing Hummer.

"Get out of my house!" she screamed.

"Gladly."

I pulled a weeping Johnathan from the sofa and walked toward the door. I stopped when I saw my mother in the doorway. "Took your ass long enough," I frowned, thinking that

Germaine's mom could've been killing me while mine sat in the car. She lifted Johnathan in her arms as we walked back to the car.

"Nikki, what are you doing?" she asked after we drove off.

I ignored her because Johnathan's crying was getting on my nerves. "Will you shut up?" I yelled at him. That only made it worse. He cried louder and harder.

"Nikki, whatever is going on with you please don't take it out on these boys."

"Well, I guess I learned from the best because you sure as hell used to take your anger out on me," I reminded her.

I turned the volume up on the radio to drown Johnathan's cries. I had too much on my mind and I didn't need him or my mother to add to it.

Chapter Twenty

"Don't answer your damn phone if Germaine calls you," I threatened my mother after securing her and my boys in at the Four Seasons. "And don't call him!"

"You need to tell me what's going on, Nikki? Why are you hiding the boys from their father?"

"I have my reasons. Just don't answer the phone if he calls."

I kissed my boys goodbye then left. As soon as I hopped in my car, I called Kingston. He needed to know what was going on.

"What's up?" he answered.

I didn't like his greeting, but what the hell. "I need to see you. We need to talk." I ranted. "When can we meet?"

"Well, actually, I'm in town now."

"Why didn't you tell me you were in town?"

"Because I'm not gonna be here long and I don't have to tell you my every fucking move."

I was blown away by his attitude. "You still should've called me." I was starting to get sick on the stomach knowing that he was damn near in arms reach and I didn't even know it.

"What's the emergency, Niquole?"

"We can't do this over the phone. I can get us a room."

"I don't have time for that."

"I wasn't asking you to fuck me, Kingston," I said in an insulted tone. "Privacy."

"I've got things I need to take care of, Niquole."

He was making this harder than it needed it to be. "Well, can you catch a later flight? Can you meet me later? This is important," I practically begged.

I could tell that he was thinking about my proposal because he was silent for a few seconds. "Where and what time?"

"What time is good for you?" I inquired.

"In a couple of hours."

"There is this park on Memorial Loop Drive near Arnot Street. It's…."

"I know where it is," he cut me off. I didn't question how he knew where the park was because I didn't care. I just needed to see him. "I'll call you when I'm on my way." Without a goodbye, he hung up.

I needed to call my mother to check on the kids, and to see if Germaine had contacted her. I needed to make sure I kept drilling in her head to not answer the phone if he called. She had a soft spot for Germaine and I needed to harden it. I knew Kingston would kill him once he found out what Germaine did to me. But I had to make sure Kingston didn't know that I initiated it. I actually wanted to be present when he took care of Germaine. I wanted to see him tied up like Hummer. I wanted to see him begging and pleading with his eyes. I wanted tears to stream down his face as he watched Kingston point a gun in his face and me on the sideline smiling. I wanted that bastard to know it was me who orchestrated his death.

I was happy that Kingston declined my invitation to get a room because I knew we'd end up having sex. I could never resist him when we were together. I would've loved to have him kissing and stroking me, but I was in no shape to have him between my legs. Germaine made sure of that. One minute he was gentle then the next he was a brute. He had me in positions that he and I had never tried before. He'd pushed me way past my limits. It was almost as if his ass was trying to make up for lost time. I thought he'd stop when he saw and heard me crying, but that shit made him push even harder, like he wanted to punish me. Like he wanted me to pay for my sins.

When my phone rang, it cleared my thoughts. I glanced at the caller ID. It was Germaine. I sent him straight to voice-mail then called my mother.

"Did he call you?" I asked as soon as she answered.

"Yes, he did."

"Why did you answer the phone? Do you know how to follow fucking directions?"

"He kept calling, Nikki. I had to."

"You didn't have to answer! What did he say?"

"He asked me had I seen you and if I had the boys."

"What did you tell him?"

"I couldn't lie to him with Nathan crying and Johnathan laughing in the background."

"Did you tell him where you were?"

"No, Nikki, I didn't. You need to tell me what's going on."

When my line beeped, I glanced at the ID. It was Meagan. What in the hell did she want? "Mama, I gotta go." I clicked over to Meagan. "What?"

"Did you forget?" she asked frantically.

"Forget what?"

"Dizzy, Flex Jones and Clarise Mason are leaving."

"Shit!" I screamed into the phone. How in the hell could I forget that they were coming to sign their contracts today? "Meagan, I'll be there in…"

"No need to, Niquole."

"What do you mean? I'll be there in like fifteen minutes."

"All three of them say they've been trying to contact you for over a week and don't feel comfortable working with you."

"No one has called me. No one has emailed me."

"Niquole, you've been out a lot lately. You haven't been giving much attention to what's been going on around here," she said like I needed a reminder.

"No one has called my fucking phone!"

"Did you give them your cell phone number? If you didn't, they've probably been calling the office and leaving messages. Have you checked them?"

"No, Meagan," I calmed down after realizing that I'd probably just lost out on three great acts. "Besides, you're my fucking assistant. If any messages or calls came through, wouldn't you be the first to get them?" I asked nastily as I thought about her involvement with Kingston.

"I…I haven't received any calls or messages either," she stuttered.

I felt like she was lying. "Meagan, if I find out that you had something to do with this shit, your ass is mine!"

"Niquole, what are you talking about?" she asked like I'd insulted and hurt her feelings. "What reason would I have to do that to you?"

Because you want my man. "Is there anything else, Meagan?"

"Yeah, there is." There was a long pause. "They're all going to A.J.'s label."

"What?" I freaked out.

"From what they're telling me, A.J. is offering them a deal they can't refuse."

"You're fucking kidding me?!" I screamed. "That sneaky bastard!"

"They gave you a chance, and…"

"Look, I don't need you to make me feel any shittier than I already feel right now. Fine! Fuck it! Tell 'em to go onto A.J. then! I don't give a shit!"

"Are you okay?"

I hung up.

It was an injury to lose out on the three acts, but them going to A.J. was a damn insult. He'd probably bad mouthed me to them, too. That son-of-a-bitch coming to the album release party was no coincidence. He'd obviously come to check out my fresh new talent and steal 'em away from me. I guess that was making me pay for what I did to him. Once I got all my shit in order, he would be hearing from me. Greedy bastard.

I couldn't believe how out of focus I had become. I never would've let something that important slip my mind. My life was getting more fucked up by the minute, but seeing Kingston was more important than anything else going on in my life. I had a few hours to kill before we met up. It quickly dawned on me that I was still in the Four Seasons parking lot. I also had worked up an appetite. I needed energy.

I drove to the nearest McDonald's, grabbed a Big Mac extra value meal then headed to the park. I sat in my car and watched the kids play and the parents converse amongst themselves. I smiled as I thought about me and Kingston doing that one day with the boys and maybe a child of our own.

I dug my hand into the bag for the loose fries that had fallen out of the holder. They were hot just like I liked them. I shoved a few in my mouth and washed them down with the Sprite that came with the meal. Out of nowhere, the sky suddenly became a little dark. A storm was brewing. Suddenly, the parents began scooping their kids and tossing them in cars. Pretty soon, the park was empty. I finished off my meal while listening to Heather Headley. I then let my seat back, and released a flood of tears. I must've been in my own little world because the next thing I knew, I heard someone knocking on my window.

"Niquole? Niquole?"

When I jumped and looked up, Kingston was standing beside the car. I took a quick glance at the dashboard clock.

"Hey," I greeted him after letting the window down.

"What did you need to talk to me about? It's about to rain and I need to get going."

I didn't like the fact that he was rushing me. I turned my car off and stepped out. It took everything in me not to dive into his arms. I needed him.

"Can I at least get a hug?" I asked thinking that was a terrible thing to ask by the look on his face.

"Niquole, what is it?" he asked. "I don't have time for this."

I walked over to one of the picnic tables and sat down. Kingston followed but stood a few feet away from me. I couldn't understand why he was acting like this especially since I hadn't told him the bad news. I braced myself and took a deep breath.

"Germaine knows that I had something to do with Hummer's death."

His eyes widened. "How in the hell does he know that?"

I stood up. "Baby, he found the jacket in the trash and he had the blood tested." I made sure not to let him know that I'd actually confessed to Germaine that the blood was Hummer's. I watched Kingston bite his bottom lip. I swallowed the huge lump in my throat. "I promise that I didn't say anything about you. He thinks I paid someone to kill him." His silence was killing me so I had to pour it on a little thicker. "Baby, he made me have sex with him. He raped me." I was pissed because I couldn't formulate any tears. "Baby, if we just go ahead and get rid of him then no one will ever know. You can leave your wife so we can be together."

He stared at me for a few seconds. "You're one stupid bitch!" he yelled right before slapping the taste out of my mouth. The blow was so hard that I fell back on the table. Stunned, I grabbed my throbbing cheek.

"Kingston. I'm sorry," I cried. There was no need for me to create fake tears anymore because these were real. "I promise you that I didn't tell him anything."

He grabbed me and got all up in my face. "How could you be so fucking stupid? I told your ass to get rid of it!" he screamed while shaking me.

"Baby, I'm sorry. It's not my fault. He saw me when I threw it away."

"Why in the fuck did you throw it away at your damn house, Niquole?" My mouth opened, but nothing came out. "You didn't get rid of it when I told you to, did you?"

"Baby, please. I forgot."

He slapped me again.

"You're taking the fall for that muthafucka's death if your bitch ass husband gets a chance to go to the police! I knew I shouldn't have fucked around with you for this long!" he ranted then paced around in circles. "I got sidetracked fucking around with you!"

"What do you mean by that?"

"This shit between you and me wasn't supposed to go on for this long."

The tears started flowing faster. "But you…you love me, Kingston."

"Bitch, please," he laughed menacingly. "I don't fucking love you."

"But you killed Hummer for me. If that's not love then what is?"

My stomach began to turn in knots as I listened to him laugh like I'd said something funny.

"I didn't kill Hummer for you, bitch. His death had nothing to do with you. It just played right into my plan to string you along, but I didn't expect for you to be this damn needy and obsessed."

"What are you saying? I don't understand."

"You were just a ploy in my plan. All of this was just a fucking act."

Those knots in my stomach twisted even more. What

was he talking about? What was he saying to me? I was confused. "I still don't understand, Kingston."

He pulled his wallet from his back pocket and pulled out a newspaper article. I stared at him in disbelief as he shoved it in my face. I read the headline.

A young woman was found brutally raped in a local club parking lot.

"What is this about?" I asked.

He pulled a photo of a girl from the wallet and shoved it in my face, too. "This is the girl they're talking about."

I still didn't understand what any of that had to do with me. "I don't get it, Kingston. Who is that?"

"This is my fucking sister!"

"Oh my God, but what does she have to do with me?"

"This happened a month before I met you. She's dead now. She killed herself because she couldn't deal with it."

"I'm sorry but what…"

"Your fucking husband and that nigga Hummer did it! They raped her!"

Shock was an understatement for me, but I couldn't help but wonder how he could possibly know they were the culprits. I was too outdone to ask him how he knew. I still couldn't get over the fact that the man who I loved was only using me. My body was weak and I felt like I could hardly breathe. When I stared into his eyes, I saw nothing but coldness. Then something hit me.

"You cut Germaine's brake line, didn't you?"

"What do you think?"

"You put the pin in my jacket."

"In case you didn't throw it away, I needed you to be the number one suspect."

I was speechless. "Did you flatten my tires at that reception?"

"Naw, I didn't do that."

Well who in the hell did that? I thought. "I still don't get it. What was your plan and how was I a part of it?"

"Please don't tell me that you're this fucking stupid. Hummer is dead, Niquole. Who do you think is next? I needed you to get close to your husband."

I stared at Kingston like he was something from out of space. I should've been really afraid of him at that moment, but I wasn't. Any other woman would've took off running like an Olympic sprinter, but I wasn't one of those women. Hell, I wanted what he wanted…Germaine dead.

"I don't care what you say, you love me. You fell in love with me Kingston."

"Let me show you just how much I love you," Kingston spoke sinisterly as he approached me.

"What do you mean? What are you doing?" I asked when he grabbed my wrists.

"I think it's only fair if that bitch ass husband of yours feels the same way I felt when he raped my sister."

Suddenly, he threw me across the picnic table and yanked my jeans to my ankles. "Kingston, what are you doing?" I cried. "I just told you that Germaine raped me."

"Then it should be easy for me to get in." He punched me in my face then forced me onto my stomach. "I'm gonna make sure you don't like this then maybe you'll leave me the hell alone," he breathed devilishly in my ear before forcing himself inside my asshole.

Chapter Twenty-One

"Ma'am? Ma'am, can you tell us what happened to you?"

I could hardly see the nurse who was asking me questions because my right eye had nearly closed from Kingston's fist.

"Ma'am did you drive yourself here?"

I was in another world that involved total disbelief and disarray, but I nodded yes after thinking back to me damn near crawling to my car. There was another butch-looking female standing on the other side of me holding a camera. Now, I knew what those rape victims on *Law & Order SVU* felt like. I think I shocked them when I refused to have a rape kit done. The nurse stared at me with disbelief. I guess she couldn't understand my reason.

"You need to let the doctor check out your wounds," she said.

"Wounds?" I asked curiously while touching my face. My eye was swollen and my lip felt split. .

"Let me get you into a room so the doctor can see you," she said in a tone like I didn't have a choice. Five minutes later, I was in a private room. "An officer should be in here shortly to take your statement, ma'am," the nurse advised me with a warm smile before exiting the room.

Once she closed the door, I lost it. "How could you do

that to me and then leave me in the rain?" I cried out loud. "You love me, Kingston! You fucking love me!" I screamed. "Baby, you hurt me, but I know you didn't mean it! It's not your fault! It's not your fucking fault!"

I couldn't get the visual out of my head. I also couldn't believe Kingston had used me as a punching bag and raped me in broad daylight. His ass being bold was an understatement. Who did shit like that in a fucking park?

When it began to rain, I thought he would stop, but he didn't. It actually intensified the moment for him. The harder he beat me, the louder I screamed. The harder he fucked me, the louder I screamed. That was what he wanted. He wanted to break me down like his sister had been. He wanted me to feel what his sister felt. He wanted to give Germaine a dose of his own medicine at my expense. The entire situation was fucked up.

I was so wrapped up in my emotions that I didn't see or hear Germaine walk into the room. His facial expressions went from concerned to terrified and apologetic, but mine stayed the same as I stared at him. Anger and disgust.

"How did you know that I was here?" I asked.

"Tyrell was dispatched to come and interview a domestic violence victim. When he saw that it was you, he called me. Nikki, baby, what happened?" Germaine asked nearly in tears. He stood beside me and reached for my hand. However, I yanked it away as I thought back to what Kingston had told me about the incident with his sister. I certainly believed it to be true. Besides, why wouldn't I believe it? Hummer had even tried to rape me and Germaine had just took advantage of me as well. They were monsters who needed to be stopped.

"Why do you care? You did the same shit to me the other night."

He gave me a look of disbelief. "I didn't rape you, Nikki. I just played along with your game."

"Call it what you want," I said then rolled my eyes. I

wanted him out of my face and out of my room. I didn't need him there trying to comfort me when he was the reason I was there.

"Who did this to you? Tell me, please," Germaine pleaded.

I glared at him. "It doesn't matter. You're not gonna do a damn thing about it anyway."

"What? I'd do anything for you, Nikki."

"My fucking name is Niquole!" I screamed demonically causing him to jump back. "This is all your fucking fault!"

"My fault? What are you talking about?" he asked confused.

All I could think about was him being the reason why Kingston was so upset. If Germaine hadn't done what he did, then things between me and Kingston would've been perfect. Not to mention, I wouldn't have been raped.

"Get out," I ordered.

"Baby, if this is about last night, I'm sorry."

"Leave! Just fucking go!"

I could tell that he was thrown for a loop by my actions. "I talked to your mom before I came here. I'm going to get the boys and take them home."

At this point, I really didn't give a damn. "Germaine, I don't care. Just leave me the hell alone."

Germaine backed away, never taking his eyes off of me. He was nearly struck by the opening of the door as he backed into it. It was Meagan carrying two dozens of yellow tulips. When she tried to hug Germaine, I saw a little hesitation on his part. That wasn't the first time I saw him act a little awkward around her.

"Okay, I'm leaving," he said before quickly hurrying out the door.

I glared at Meagan. I didn't want her near me. "Meagan, how did you know I was here?"

"My cousin works here. She called me."

I could only imagine who else knew I was in the hospital. I watched Meagan as she walked toward me. This bitch had some nerve. As soon as she reached me, she burst into tears. I wondered if I looked that bad or if she was feeling guilty about something.

"I'm so sorry, Niquole. I had no clue he would do this to you."

I sat up straight in the bed and stared at her with curious eyes. "What are you talking about? Who are you talking about?"

"Kingston. I didn't know he would hurt you like this."

My eyes widened. "Whoa! Back the fuck up! What the hell is going on? How in the hell do you know Kingston?"

"Kingston's sister was my best friend."

I reached for a cup of water from the table beside me when I started choking on nothing. "Excuse me?" I asked after getting myself together.

"I was there the night she was raped. She told me she was going outside to talk to a friend. When she was gone for a while, I went outside to check on her, but she was nowhere to be found. That's when I heard noises on the side of the club. Me, being the nosey person I am, I walked in that direction and immediately covered my mouth at what I saw. Germaine was holding her down while his friend covered her mouth and raped her. When I screamed, they fled."

I was completely shocked as Meagan kept going.

"That guy, Hummer, dropped his wallet and I got the license plate of Germaine's truck. I was gonna give the information to the police, but Kingston told me not to. He did research on Hummer and Germaine and found out that Germaine was married to you and that you were looking for a new assistant. That day I came in to talk to you, you had an emergency call that you needed to take and walked out of the office. You had several resumes and portfolios on your desk in piles of *yes* and *no*. I made sure mine stuck out before slipping a few of the potential candidates in the *no* pile. That emergency call wasn't real. Kingston needed me on the inside."

I was waiting for Ashton Kutcher to jump out from the bathroom because I was more than sure that I was being punked in the worse way. Now, I knew why she was calling Kingston.

"You conniving, white bitch!" I yelled. I tried to lunge at her, but was in too much pain. I wanted her head on a stake.

She laughed creepily after stepping away from me.

Wow…from tears to psychotic in a matter of seconds, I thought. What was really going on? "What's so damn funny?" I asked.

"I've been practicing those tears for the past hour," she continued laughing. "Word of advice, if you go the police about any of this, Kingston has photos of you at Hummer's crime scene and he knows where you live," she threatened.

I was speechless as I watched and listened to that blonde bitch laugh at me. She was having the time of her life. She even flaunted that Louis Vuitton bag that I'd bought her as a pre-bribe. All along she was playing me with the man I was trying to bribe her with. I trusted her. I gave her complete access into my world and she'd played me like a fiddle.

Meagan walked to the door then turned around to face me, "Germaine deserves whatever Kingston has planned for him because my friend didn't deserve what they did to her." She shook her head. "Oh, before I go, I have one question for you."

"Bitch, what could you possibly have to ask me?" I growled.

"How does it feel to know that you bought that Prada dress for the album release party and not Kingston?"

My heart crumbled. She'd obviously used my money to buy the dress. "You bitch."

"Did it feel good when you fucked him in it?"

The more she spoke, my insides damn near exploded.

"He does know his way around a woman's pussy, doesn't he?" she questioned. "Trust me, I know."

I forced back vomit. "Why? Why did you do this? I gave you everything. I let you into my fucking world and treated you like family!"

"At first, I felt a little sorry for what we were going to do to you. I actually didn't want to do it, but as I got to know you, I realized you were a bitch. By the way, I did erase those messages those three artists left for you and I'm the one who told A.J. about them."

I couldn't stop staring at her. I wanted to rip her eyes out. This bitch had sold me out in more ways than one.

"I'll leave you alone now to ponder over everything. Oh, by the way, thanks for the money," she winked.

"What? What money?"

A crooked smile sliced across her face then she walked out. Seconds later, it hit me. She was the blackmailer. "You bitch!" I screamed.

Chapter Twenty-Two

The next morning, I sat in my hospital bed impatiently waiting for my release papers. I wanted to get away from the cops, nurses and doctors. They were getting on my damn nerves. I also needed to get out of there to find Meagan because she was due a well-whooped ass. There was no way she was getting away with her involvement and my money.

The cops were in and out of my room trying to get answers regarding my rape as they called it. However, I wasn't telling them a damn thing about Kingston because I needed some answers. Besides, if I told on him I knew he would turn me in and I wasn't having that. *All of this would've never happened if Germaine and Hummer hadn't touched Kingston's sister,* I thought. *None of this shit would be going on. My man and I would be together right now. This could've been an easy transition.*

I couldn't find it in my heart to hate Kingston for what he did. He wanted pay back and I could understand that. I didn't give a damn what Kingston said, I knew he loved me. It may have started off as a plot at first, but we spent too much time together for him not to feel the same way about me as I did. He needed some convincing.

As I sat and waited for the doctor, I wondered who in the hell leaked to the press that I had been assaulted because a few of them had found their way to my room. I figured it had to be Meagan. I even had security escort the vulchers out and stand outside my door just to get some peace. I couldn't wait to get my hands on Meagan. Her ass was surely gonna pay.

"This shit is taking too long," I said before hopping off the bed and walking toward the door. As soon as I opened it, the nurse was standing there holding my release forms.

"I thought I was gonna have to release my damn self," I pouted.

"I'm sorry about the wait, Ms. Wright. There was a…"

"I don't care. Just release me so I can get out of these damn scrubs." I frowned thinking I could be wearing them for the next twenty-five years if shit didn't go my way.

"I just need you to sign these forms," the nurse said as she handed them to me as well as a pen. "Are you sure you don't want to speak with a rape counselor?"

"Yes, I'm sure. Can I leave?" I asked sternly.

"Of course."

She nodded, smiled weakly, retrieved the papers and walked out. I was five seconds behind her. I shook my head when I saw that the guard was no longer at the door. "Where the fuck is he?" I asked myself before hearing the sound of high heels click against the floor. I had a funny suspicion whom they might've belonged to. Seconds later, I was staring at a pair of navy blue, Manolo Blahnik pumps. My suspicions were right.

"Are you okay?" Jalisa asked once I looked up at her. "Germaine called and told me to come and get you."

"Damn! Who else has he told?"

"The man is worried about you. I'm worried about you."

I shook my head. "Whatever. I've gotta get out of here. I need to find my keys."

"Actually Germaine had Tyrell drive your car home. He sent me to pick you up and take you home."

"I'm not going back there," I replied, thinking back to

that awful night with Germaine. I was never stepping foot back inside that house while he was there. "I'll catch a cab to a hotel."

"Why don't you wanna go home?"

"Ask Germaine why I don't wanna go home."

Jalisa gave me a curious look, but didn't question me. "Nikki, I'll take you to a hotel if that's what you need."

I thought against it, but figured my trip would be quicker if she drove me rather than waiting for a cab. "Okay," I sighed, knowing that she was going to question me the entire drive.

As we walked toward the elevator, I could feel someone creeping behind us. I turned around abruptly. It was the nurse who'd just left my room. My abrupt turn startled her. She was holding up her camera phone. I assume she was taking pictures of me when I suddenly thought about something. I'd completely forgotten about Meagan telling me that her cousin worked there. Was she Meagan's cousin? She gave me a frightened look when I walked up to her.

"Is Meagan your cousin?" I asked in a pleasant tone to throw her off.

"Yes," she answered.

At that moment, I snatched the phone from her hand and smashed it to the floor. It shattered in several pieces throughout the hall. "You won't have me on Youtube or in the tabloids, bitch," I growled at her.

"Come on, Nikki. Let's go," Jalisa said after clutching my arm and pulling me out of the girl's face.

We hopped inside her 2009 Mercedes CLS when we made it to the parking lot. As soon as we drove off, she started. "So, are you going to tell me what happened?"

"No, I'm not," I answered quickly.

"Look. I know we've been butting heads since forever, but you're still my friend. We've been through a lot of shit, Nikki. Talk to me. Tell me what happened."

"If Germaine had kept his dick in his pants then none of this would've happened," I responded.

"What in the world are you talking about, Nikki? Do you know who did this to you?" Jalisa looked confused.

"This is Germaine's fault."

I groaned when she pulled off the road. She obviously wasn't going to leave it alone. "You know who raped you, don't you?" Jalisa asked. I didn't respond. I figured if I ignored her that she would eventually drive off, but who was I kidding? "Have you talked to Kingston? Have you told him what happened?"

"I don't have to since he's the one who raped me and Germaine is to blame for it!" I yelled.

She gave me a freaked out look. "I can't believe what you just said."

"Just leave it alone."

"What are you doing?" Jalisa asked when she saw me grab her Droid phone from the cup holder. "We need to talk about this, Nikki. This is some serious shit."

I ignored her and continued dialing the number. "Shit!" I yelled when my call went straight to voicemail. I dialed it again and again. I was frantic and Jalisa could tell.

"Who are you trying to call?" she pried.

"Kingston! Who in the hell do you think? I need to talk to him!" I screamed.

I could tell that she was completely floored. "Have you lost your fucking mind? You can't be this strung out over this man?"

If only she knew how strung out I was. But there was more to our relationship than just that. I shushed her when my fourth call didn't go directly to voicemail.

"Hello?"

There was brief laughter, but I knew who'd just answered. "Meagan?"

"May I help you?" she laughed again.

"You trifling whore!"

"Look who's calling the kettle black."

"Where is he? Where is my Kingston?"

"*Your* Kingston?

"Put him on the phone, bitch! You better hope I don't run into your ass anytime soon."

"Whatever," she said in a nonchalant tone.

"Put Kingston on the damn phone!" I screamed.

"Hold on a second. Let me get him for you."

During the ten second wait, I could've filled a bucket with the tears that poured out of my eyes.

"Yeah?" Kingston spoke when he got on the phone.

"Baby, please don't hang up on me," I begged. I fumed when I heard him and Meagan whispering and laughing about how stupid I was. Their actions truly pissed me off. "We really need to talk, Kingston."

"About what?" he replied. "This is over."

"Over? Over?" I asked rhetorically. "Well, how do you think your wife would feel if she found out about us?" I threatened.

"Sweetheart, that chic that you saw me with is not *my* wife."

My eyes widened. "Not your wife? Who was she then? Why was she crying at the reception about Hummer being dead?"

"She was his cousin. Since he didn't have a sister, I had to fuck the next best thing. I ended up taking care of the nigga before I got the chance to torture her though."

"So, you used her to get to him?"

"Yeah. She served her purpose just like you did," he boldly stated. "She ended up having good pussy so I kept her around for fun."

"But you wear a wedding ring, Kingston."

"Sweetheart, I'm not married. I just like the ring. Now, stop fucking calling me."

Click.

I stared at the phone for a few seconds, then in a fit of rage I began smashing it on the dashboard.

The next afternoon, I found myself sitting in a king-sized bed at the Westin Galleria staring at the black television screen. I'd been sitting that way for hours as my mind raced a million miles per minute. The last thing I remembered was Jalisa cursing me out for breaking her phone and denting her dashboard. It wouldn't have shocked me if the airbag had deployed because that's how hard I'd hit it. It felt like I had the strength of a three-hundred pound man.

When Jalisa drove me to the hotel, she didn't even bother to wait until I was safe in my room. Instead, her ass sped away as soon as my feet were no longer inside the car. I don't know why she took *my* business so fucking personal in the first place.

When I received my key, I went straight to my room for a much needed shower. Even though I also needed some fresh clothes to change into, that task would just have to wait until I got myself together. Besides, there was no way I would be going to anybody's mall looking like this. If I needed anything in the meantime, the hotel gift shop would just have to do for now.

As soon as I closed the door to my room, I began to strip and headed straight for the bathroom. Turning on the water and almost immediately hopping inside, all I could think about was wringing Meagan's neck. That bitch needed to pay for her involvement. After slaughtering her in my thoughts, Germaine and Hummer entered.

Why in the hell would they rape someone, I wondered. As much as I didn't want to admit it, I knew it was true. I couldn't help but speculate if the two of them had ever raped anyone else and if that's what Hummer meant by *sharing*. The thought turned my stomach. *Who in the hell did I marry*? As thoughts about Germaine continued to disgust me, soon it wasn't going to matter anyway because Kingston was going to get rid of him. Actually, Germaine deserved whatever was coming his way for what he'd done to my man's sister. Now, I knew why he didn't beat Hummer's ass when he assaulted me that night. Maybe Germaine's sick ass got off on that shit, too. He surely seemed to get off while forcing himself on me.

Giving myself a thorough cleaning, I turned off the shower and climbed out. I didn't bother to dry off after seeing my face in the mirror. No wonder people were staring at me. Not only was my eye swollen, but my lip was busted and cheek appeared severely bruised. Kingston had really done a number on me.

I walked out of the bathroom then to the bed, dripping water on the floor. Then I laid across the plush, white comforter thinking about Kingston. What other woman in her right mind would still be in love with a man who'd raped her? What other woman would still want him? *Me*, I thought. I was crazy for still loving and wanting him, but couldn't help myself. I was in love with him and was going get him no matter the costs.

I reached for the phone on the nightstand and dialed my mother's number. At this point, I didn't know where my boys were, but they should've been with her. While the phone rang, I started tripping about the fact that she hadn't even bothered to call or come by the hospital to check on me. That was the type of relationship that she and I had; a fucked up one. She finally answered. I'm sure it took her a while since she didn't recognize the number.

"Hello?"

"Do you still have my boys?" I asked, wasting no time. There was a long pause like she was trying to figure out what to say. "Don't get quiet on me now. You think I'm pissed off because you didn't come by or call?" I asked with a slight laugh. "Don't worry about it. I neither expected you to nor did I want you to," I continued.

"Are you okay?" she asked in what seemed to me like a forced, sympathetic tone.

"Don't act like you give a shit about me. Do you have my boys?"

"No," she answered bluntly. That concern disappeared quickly. "Germaine picked them up last night."

"I specifically told you not to answer your phone when he called."

"He left me a message about what happened to you. I had no other choice but to call him. I'm not gonna be in the middle of this bullshit that you more than likely started. Those boys need their father and he needs them."

"Are you still at the hotel?" I asked.

"Yeah," she answered.

"Well, you may wanna leave because I'm about to call the front desk and tell them that you're checking out. Your ass is no longer needed right now. Go back home."

Click.

There was no need for me to argue with my mother, especially when her ass was always on Germaine's side. I took a deep breath as I contemplated calling him. I knew it was gonna be hard to control myself and keep what I knew at bay, but I had to talk to him to find out about my boys. I dialed his cell. No answer. When I dialed the house phone, he picked up on the first ring.

"Yeah?" He sounded pissed.

"Why did you take Johnathan and Nathan from my

mom?"

"Nikki?" Germaine asked like he wanted to make sure it was me.

"Yeah. Where are the boys?"

"Who in the hell is Kingston?" he blasted and flipped the script.

I didn't expect that question and I damn sure wasn't prepared to answer. "Wh…Who?" I stammered, trying to buy some time. I needed to figure out how in the hell he knew about my man.

"Don't play dumb with me, Nikki!" he yelled. "Jalisa told me about him!"

What? That bitch, I thought. "I don't know what Jalisa told you, but…"

"She told me everything! You've been fucking with that nigga since you were pregnant with Nathan! That's why you stopped fucking me!"

I was floored and couldn't believe that bitch had sold me out.

"And he's the same nigga who raped you!" Germaine continued. "What the fuck is that all about?"

I couldn't take it any longer. "If you must know, I stopped fucking you because you fucked with my pills! You caused me to get pregnant when your ass knew that I didn't want any more damn kids! And as far as Kingston raping me goes, it's your damn fault he did it! He raped me because you raped his fucking sister!"

Germaine paused for a few seconds. "What in the hell are you talking about?"

"Like you just told me…don't play dumb. You and Hummer raped his fucking sister and she killed herself because of it." Germaine was silent as I kept going. "While you're thinking back to it, throw this in your thoughts as well. I want out of this fucked-up-ass marriage! You ain't about shit! I hate you! There's no telling how many girls you and Hummer have raped!"

"I didn't rape anybody, Nikki!"

"There's no need for you to lie. Meagan was there and....Oh my God! Now, it all makes sense why you were always nervous around her. You saw her! That's why you didn't want me to hire her!"

If a pin had dropped, it would've been heard.

"I didn't rape her, Hummer did," Germaine finally said. "Besides, I never really knew if Meagan was the girl from that night. She looked familiar, but I wasn't a hundred percent sure. Because of that, I didn't like being around her."

"So, what did you do just watch like a fucking pervert?"

"This isn't about me. This is about you!"

"Seems to me that it's about the both of us!"

"Let me remind you that I know you had something to do with Hummer's murder. If any of this shit gets out, I can go to the cops, Nikki."

Was he really playing that card? I had one to play, too. "So can I, asshole! I'm sure that girl's case is still open since neither you nor Hummer got locked up."

"I didn't rape her. I...I just held her down."

"And that makes you a fucking saint?" I asked sarcastically. "You assisted in her rape. I can go to the cops!"

"You can go to the cops on me all you want. Did you forget that Tyrell and a few of my other frat brothers are cops? Any evidence would be destroyed just like it was then."

Wow. I couldn't believe that all this time, I'd been married to the devil. Germaine was right. As long as he had friends on the force, he'd probably never be prosecuted.

"I'm not living like this with you anymore, Germaine. I don't want you. I want to be with Kingston. You'll never get a chance to turn me in for Hummer's murder because Kingston is going to kill you just like he did Hummer." I knew it was dumb to let Germaine know that I was somewhat involved in

Hummer's murder, but I didn't give a damn anymore. His ass needed to know that his days were numbered.

That comment didn't sit well with him. "You trifling bitch! That nigga killed my friend and you knew about it?"

"Hummer had to pay for his sins against me as well as Kingston's sister and you're next," I spoke boldly.

"You think you got this shit all figured out, don't you?" he laughed. "Let me make you this promise. You won't get the chance to be happy with that nigga because I'll get Tyrell to handle him. And if you get in my fucking way, you'll be handled as well!"

Click.

Did he just threaten me? My fingers went numb as the phone traveled down my chest to the bed. If there was truly such a thing as the perfect storm, I was sitting right in the middle of it.

After picking up a few outfits from the mall the next day, I called Jalisa and asked her to take me to the label. Not only had I been neglecting my business, but more importantly, I wanted to see that bitch so I could give her an earful about snitching on me to Germaine. She tried to get out of picking me up, but when I ended up begging her, she eventually caved in. I made sure not to let on that I knew she'd sold me out. I wanted to drop that bombshell on her when we were face to face.

Fifteen minutes later, Jalisa called to tell me that she was downstairs, but I was already in the lobby waiting for her. I walked outside and stepped slowly toward her car. I could tell she was worried. After getting inside, I decided to torture her a little while longer.

"How are you feeling?" she asked.

I forced back the evil stare that I was prepared to give her. "I'm good." I shifted my body and stared out the window. If she wanted to talk, she was gonna have to speak to the back of my head because I had no words for her. Not right now anyway.

After trying to talk to me for the entire twenty-five minute trip and only receiving one word answers, Jalisa never gave up. Even when we arrived at the label, she walked with me inside. It was almost as if she was determined to see what I had on my mind. However, at that point, I had to put my issues with her to the side, because I was stunned to find the office totally vacant. Looking around the deserted hallways, there was no one in sight. Even the studios were empty, which was rare because someone was always working on music. Shaking my head, I figured Meagan's bitch ass had something to do with everyone being MIA.

"Damn, did you give everyone the day off?" Jalisa asked. "I'll be right back. I need to use the restroom."

I didn't bother to reply since I was still shocked and confused as to why no one was working. I walked to Meagan's desk and frowned when I saw that it was completely bare; almost as if it was never occupied. No phone, no files, no pens…nothing. The bitch had cleared everything out even the laptop that didn't belong to her.

I was just about to open one of the drawers to see if it was empty as well, when a noise from my office startled me. I wondered who in the hell could've be in there. Even though I hadn't been to the label in days, my office was always off- limits…period.

I tiptoed to the door so whoever was inside wouldn't hear me. After opening it slightly, I gasped when I saw Meagan vigorously tapping on my Mac keyboard and Kingston opening and closing desk drawers.

"What the hell are y'all doing here?" I glared mostly at Meagan because I desperately wanted to beat that bitches ass.

They both stopped abruptly.

"What the fuck are y'all doing here?" I asked again after scouring the room.

Meagan's face had turned fire engine red and her eyes went back and forth from me to Kingston as if she were waiting for one of us to make the first move. Mine however locked on my computer that she was standing in front of. Not only did I have confidential employee information stored on there, but I also had my company bank records as well as all my credit card information just in case I lost one of my cards. Is that what they wanted? Even though I trusted Meagan at one point, nobody had the password to my Mac. I'm sure she thought it was KINGSTON like on my home computer, and other important stuff, but at the label I always used BISHOP…my beloved father's nick name.

With every step I made toward her, Meagan made two steps back. "Why the fuck are you at my computer?" I addressed her. When I finally reached my desk and looked at the screen, there was an error message stating that the password was incorrect.

I looked up at Meagan who'd backed up against the wall by now. "So what bitch, all that money I gave you wasn't good enough? You looking for more?"

Meagan stared back and forth from me to Kingston. That bitch had a mouth on her at the hospital and even over the phone, but now all that shit had changed. She seemed afraid. She needed to be.

"Answer me, bitch!" I demanded.

"You deal with this shit, Kingston," Meagan addressed him with a hint of fear in her voice. "I told you this was a bad idea."

"Shut the fuck up!" he scowled at her. "Go wait in the fucking car."

Meagan immediately gave him a look to show that she didn't appreciate the way he was talking to her, but obeyed anyway. She kept a far distance from me as she glided toward the door. I kept a death stare on her until she was gone. I slowly turned back to Kingston as he stood there in his dark-wash Rock & Republic jeans. The look on his face made me feel as though I'd invaded his office instead of the other way around.

"What are you doing here, Kingston?" I said in a soft voice.

He stood before me with a stern look on his face.

"Since you've been out of the office for a while I thought I'd try and get Meagan to see what you had on your computer. You know something we could cash in on. Maybe write a company check," he blurted out. "Do you know that dumb bitch has blown all the money she got from you? I knew I shouldn't have trusted her to keep it."

I gave him a look of disapproval and shock. I appreciated his honesty, but never thought he was a thief on top of a rapist.

"So, did you all tell my staff not to come to work?" I questioned.

"Meagan did. How else were we gonna be in your office without anyone knowing? We've been trying to crack your computer code for two days now."

When I walked toward him, Kingston put his hands up like he wanted me to stop, but I kept going. Instead, I got right up in his face. "You don't have to steal from me Kingston. I would've given you money if you'd just asked."

He smiled. "You can't be this fucking crazy. You really don't get this shit do you?"

"I do get it, baby," I whined. "You love me just like I love you."

At that point, Kingston pushed me away. "You're sick, Niquole."

"You told me that you didn't expect to be involved with me for this long. Well, that was because you fell in love with me. I don't understand why you keep denying it."

"I'm not denying it. Don't you get it? Bitch, how many times do we have to go through this shit? I never loved you. I was only with you to get back at your punk ass husband. Hell, your pussy wasn't even that good, if you want me to be real honest right now. I've had better."

It felt like someone had ripped my heart out and stomped on it. I couldn't believe Kingston was saying such horrible things to me.

"How dare you talk to me like that? After what you just put me through, I at least deserve to be shown some respect. I could've had you locked up! Hell, you could've been locked up ever since the Hummer incident. Don't you see how much I care about you?"

Kingston seemed furious. "Shut the fuck up! Your dumb ass is always talking nonsense. Maybe I should've got rid of your ass, too."

"Niquole, what's going on?"

Kingston and I turned toward the door to find Jalisa standing there with a perturbed look on her face.

"Jalisa, this is none of your business. I can handle this," I tried to convince.

"Who is this?" she asked while sizing Kingston up.

I didn't answer, but the look on her face was assurance that she knew. "I'm calling the cops," she warned while pulling her cell phone from her purse.

"That's not a good idea," Kingston threatened as he slowly approached her with a menacing look on his face.

To my and Kingston's surprise, Jalisa quickly pulled her chrome plated nine millimeter out of her purse and pointed it at him.

"Whoa!" Kingston gasped after throwing his hands up in defeat and backing away.

"Jalisa, what the fuck are you doing?" I panicked while glancing back and forth from my friend to my lover.

"Call the fucking police, Nikki!" she screamed at me. "I know who the fuck this is. You need to tell them that this son-of-a-bitch raped you!"

"Jalisa, calm down! Put that fucking gun away!" I yelled.

As soon as Jalisa took her eyes off of Kingston for one brief second, he made his move and charged her. I watched the two of them tussle back and forth for a few seconds until suddenly I heard a loud pop. My eyes were fixated on the smoke oozing from the barrel as Jalisa quickly threw the gun on the floor like she didn't have anything to do with it. By that time, Kingston was bent over in pain.

I panicked. "Oh my God. What did you do?"

"Are you fucking kidding me?" Jalisa asked like she was appalled by my actions. "He probably would've killed us if he'd gotten his hands on the gun!"

I didn't have time to respond because my attention soon turned to Kingston when I heard him moan. "Kingston, baby don't worry, I'm gonna get you help!"

As far as I could tell, he'd been shot in the shoulder. The right side of his orange, polo shirt was filled with blood. As I went to see if he was okay, suddenly Kingston pushed me out of the way, grabbed the gun and pointed it directly at Jalisa.

"You stupid bitch. Never put the gun down," Kingston taunted.

"Kingston, noooooooo!" I shouted.

"Fuck that, this bitch shot me," he replied.

"You know it was self-defense, Nikki." Jalisa's voice trembled. "Can't you see what kind of man he is? Don't let this asshole get away with what he did to you," she scolded.

"You got a lot of mouth for a bitch who has a gun pointed at her," Kingston threatened.

Jalisa stood her ground. "If you were gonna shoot me, you would've done it already."

"Call the cops, Niquole," Kingston addressed me with a sinister smile. "We'll see who they believe."

"But it was self-defense, Kingston," I said. "You were…"

"I said call the damn cops!" he yelled.

I picked up the phone on my desk, dialed 911 and frantically explained what happened before requesting an ambulance be sent as quickly as possible.

"Who the fuck are you anyway? I don't know many

bitches who walk around with guns in their purse," Kingston said to Jalisa as I hung up the phone.

I didn't even allow her to answer before I interrupted. "The operator said to apply pressure to your wound to try and control the bleeding."

"Niquole, you're one stupid ass bitch." Jalisa spoke through gritted teeth. "This man has caused so much havoc in your life and you're sitting here giving him advice like a concerned parent. He raped you!"

"He wouldn't have done it if Germaine hadn't raped his sister."

"What?" she asked surprised.

"Yes, Germaine raped his sister so Kingston decided to retaliate."

Jalisa shook her head. "I don't believe you. Germaine would never do something like that."

"Well, you need to believe me because it's true. Germaine is not a fucking saint," I replied.

When Jalisa took a few steps forward, Kingston waved the gun. "Back the fuck up!" he yelled.

"How can you wanna be with somebody like him?" Jalisa screamed.

"Because I love him and I know he loves me. We just need to get back on track once all of this shit blows over," I responded.

"Nikki, you need some help. Serious help. Can't you see that he doesn't want you? You can't keep doing this. Your father isn't coming back and you're not gonna find the love that you got from him by trying to manipulate all these men."

I scowled at her. "Shut up, Jalisa!"

"It's true and you know it!"

Kingston looked back and forth at us like he was enjoying the show.

I wanted to grab the gun and shoot her ass my damn self for bringing up my father. It was my mother's fault that he'd left in the first place. She ran him away and 'til this day, I still didn't know why. That's why I resented her. I began looking for that father figure when she would bring her boyfriends around, but my motives soon steered in another direction. I hated her for making my father leave, so I needed her to pay. I started sleeping with her men, but the pattern was always the same. They'd love me then leave me and I wasn't having that anymore. I had to make them realize that they did actually love me…starting with Kingston.

"How the fuck could you sell me out to Germaine? Why in the fuck did you tell him about Kingston?"

"Because this shit needed to stop," Jalisa replied in a bold tone. "You gotta stop hurting people Nikki."

At that moment I finally gave her an assuring expression. "Yeah, I know."

I was happy when the sirens outside ended our conversation. When Kingston finally put the gun down, I made my way over to Jalisa and hugged her. I wanted my friend to know that everything would be okay.

Soon, my office was filled with two female officers and two EMTs rolling a gurney and carrying medical bags. They didn't waste any time hurrying over to Kingston.

"Can someone tell me what happened here?" one of the female officers asked.

I faced Jalisa and smiled wickedly. It was time for her to pay for what she did to me. "She shot him," I pointed at my friend. Her eyes widened in disbelief.

The officer glanced at Jalisa then turned to Kingston who was now lying on the gurney. "Is that true, sir?' she asked him.

"Yeah, that bitch shot me," he replied.

When the officer walked over to Jalisa, I smiled after hearing the next set of words. "You have the right to remain silent. Anything you say can and will be used against you in a court of law."

"Nikki, tell them! Tell them that it was self-defense!" Jalisa ranted. "He was going to attack me! Tell them, Nikki…tell them!"

I watched as the officer placed Jalisa's hands behind her back and slapped the handcuffs around her wrists. My attention soon turned to Kingston. When I noticed the EMTs preparing to wheel him out, I rushed to his side. I passed Jalisa on my way and before walking out, I whispered to her. "That's what you get for trying to sell me out, bitch."

She tussled with the officer trying to get at me as I gave her one final sinister grin. When we made it to the ambulance, I waited for the EMTs to secure Kingston inside before I hopped in. Little did I know, Kingston had other ideas.

"No!" he yelled when I tried to climb inside. The chubby EMT looked at him. "I don't want her here," Kingston addressed.

My heart sank. The EMT looked at me then shook his head and apologized with his eyes.

"Can you at least tell me what hospital you're taking him to?" I asked.

"Noooooo," Kingston moaned again before grabbing his shoulder. This time it looked like he was in serious pain.

He was out of luck. When the driver appeared from the side of the ambulance to close the door, he advised the other EMT what hospital they were going to.

Suddenly, my thoughts quickly jumped to Meagan. After Kingston told her to wait in the car, I just knew she would be running up to him at any moment once she saw him on the stretcher. I scanned the parking lot, but surprisingly didn't see anyone's car except for Jalisa's. *That's right, bitch. You better hide.*

"I'll see you at the hospital, baby," I said despite Kingston's disapproval.

As I watched the ambulance pull off, the two female officers approached me.

"Ma'am, we need to take your statement," one of them said.

When I glanced inside the police car, Jalisa was in the back seat sobbing. Then suddenly our eyes locked. She shook her head at me then went on a complete rampage. She even screamed things at me that I couldn't hear because the window was rolled up. *I wonder if that bitch can do a photo shoot from prison*, I thought.

"What do you need to know?" I asked the officer.

I spent nearly ten minutes telling them what happened. As they pulled off, I could make out the words that were spewing from Jalisa's lips. "You're gonna get yours, bitch!"

"Yeah, that's what they all say," I spewed back.

Chapter Twenty-Five

I drove around in Jalisa's car for nearly three hours. I wanted to go to the hospital to see Kingston, but decided against it. I figured he may've been in surgery and would need some time to recuperate. Not only did I not want to put any extra strain on him, but I also needed him to be nice and calm by the time I got there.

Johnathan and Nathan quickly popped in my head once I killed the idea of going to the hospital. I hadn't had any real time with them since the drama in my life quadrupled, and I wanted to see my boys. No, I needed to see my boys. They were the only ones who brought simplicity in my life. I knew I was going to have a drag out fight with Germaine when I showed my face at the house, but I was ready to face him.

When I pulled into the driveway, Tyrell's F150 was parked there as well. I wondered what the hell he was doing at my house, but figured Germaine was more than likely telling him about Kingston. They'd become just like two gossiping bitches lately. After parking the car, I walked to the front door.

"Shit!" I yelled out after realizing that I didn't have my keys.

It didn't matter though because not even five seconds later, Germaine yanked the door open. I assumed he must've seen me pull up. He looked like a maniac as he clutched my arm and pulled me inside the house and into the living room.

"Get your fucking hands off me!" I yelled at him. I

tried to get away, but his hold was too strong. "Let me go!" I screamed just before spitting in his face.

At that moment, Germaine stopped then slapped the shit out of me.

"What the hell did you do to Jalisa?" he barked at me when I fell back on the sofa.

I noticed Tyrell standing on the other side of the room with his arms folded across his chest. He was quiet. I'm sure he already knew the answer.

"Fuck Jalisa!" I yelled then clutched my throbbing face.

"She called me and told me everything!" Germaine continued.

"She used her one phone call to call you?" I questioned.

"Does it fucking matter?" Germaine asked.

Suddenly, I started wondering where my boys were. I knew he wouldn't be acting in such a way if they were home. "Where's Johnathan and…"

Germaine cut me off. "They're not here! Now, answer the fucking question!"

"I'm not answering a damn thing! Fuck you and fuck her!" I yelled after jumping up in his face.

Germaine shoved me back onto the sofa before turning to Tyrell as if he could make me speak. Moments later, Tyrell walked toward me like his buff ass was going to intimidate me.

"Niquole, what happened at your label? What did that nigga say?" he asked after unfolding his arms.

I didn't speak a word or flinch. My lips were sealed.

"How the fuck can you defend a nigga who raped you?" Germaine barked.

"The same fucking way you tried to defend Hummer when he tried to rape me!" I rolled my neck.

Germaine didn't have a comeback so Tyrell intervened.

"What did he tell you about the rape, Niquole?" Tyrell

spoke in a soft tone.

"All I know is that Germaine and Hummer raped his sister."

"I didn't rape his fucking sister!" Germaine screamed.

"You may as well have. You held her down while your friend did it," I shot back.

Before I knew it, Germaine lunged at me. He lifted me off the sofa by my neck, dragged me to the wall and pinned me against it. His eyes were filled with anger and betrayal as he choked me and banged my head against the wall.

"If I go to fucking jail, you're going, too!" he screamed at me.

Tyrell rushed over to him and pried himself between us causing Germaine to release his hold. As I fought for air, Germaine raced upstairs, leaving Tyrell to lecture me.

Tyrell shook his head. "I told Germaine that he should've gotten rid of you a long time ago when he used to tell me about all the shit you did."

"Fuck you, fat bastard! I hope Kingston kills your ass, too!" As soon as I lashed at him, the bastard backhanded me.

Tyrell smiled. "I've wanted to do that for a long time."

I stayed on the floor. Now, I was afraid because if he had the means of getting rid of evidence, he probably had the means of getting rid of bodies. He stood over me like a prison guard, causing me to keep my mouth shut.

For about five minutes, we listened to Germaine rustle around upstairs. I wondered what he was doing. When he finally appeared, I watched him bounce down the stairs carrying two of my suitcases.

"Get the fuck out!" he yelled after dropping the bags on the floor.

I couldn't believe my ears. I scurried to my feet. "This is my damn house," I reminded him."If anyone is leaving, it's going to be you and that goon ass friend of yours!"

Germaine turned to Tyrell who immediately grabbed

me then tossed my ass out the front door. My suitcases followed.

Germaine stood in the doorway. "You can have your fucking divorce. I'm taking the boys since you don't seem to give a shit about them anyway."

"You're not..." I tried to say.

"Shut the hell up! You better keep your damn mouth shut about anything dealing with that fucking rape. Tyrell is gonna get Jalisa off for that bullshit ass charge against your *boyfriend* and *you will* retract your statement."

I frowned. "Retract it for what? She shot him!"

Germaine pointed at me like a strict teacher. "She was defending your ass and you know it."

"That bitch sold me out. She deserves whatever she gets."

"Let me say this to you and I want you to hear me loud and clear. If any of this shit falls back on me, you better watch your fucking back, Nikki," Germaine threatened.

I stood speechless. He was about to slam the door but stopped. What more could he possibly have to say to me?

"By the way, I figured *Kingston* must've been the passcode to your computer after Jalisa told me about you and him. I also figured out how you came up with Kingquole as your record label name. That was seriously foul."

I snapped my neck. "And?"

A wicked smile cut across his face. "Well, maybe you should've changed that code on your *secret* bank account. But don't worry I'm sure your conniving ass has some other money stashed away."

After that statement, he slammed the door. I ran to the door and began kicking, screaming and banging. This went one for nearly five minutes. "You better give me my damn money back, you sorry son-of-a-bitch! That's not your money, Germaine!"

When I realized I wasn't getting inside and he wasn't

coming back out, I stopped. Germaine may've thought he'd won the battle, but I would definitely be back. I was just about to retrieve my bags when I heard Tyrell and Germaine talking. That's when I pressed my ear to the door to listen. Once I heard Tyrell tell Germaine not to worry about anything and that Kingston wouldn't make it through the night, my eyes increased. Once I found out what the fuck was going on with my money, Kingston had to be warned.

Chapter Twenty-Six

I immediately rushed over to the nearest Wachovia to see if it was true. I swerved into the bank's parking lot like a drunk driver causing a few pedestrians to stare at me. However, I could care less. I was on a mission. After hopping out of the car, I rushed inside.

"Welcome to Wachovia. How may I help you today?" the metro-sexual looking white guy at the lobby desk asked. For a man he was way too skinny.

"I need to find out why you assholes allowed my money to be taken from my account without my permission."

His helpful smile slowly disappeared as he looked around at the other customers.

"Don't look at them. I'm the one who needs help!" I snapped.

"Ummm...all of the Financial Specialists are busy."

"I don't have time to wait. Can't you look into the system?" I looked at his sign. "Are you Matthew?"

He shook his head. "Yes."

"Well, it says that you're the bank manager so now I know you can help."

"Let me try and find out what's going on," he replied in an uneasy tone. "Do you have your account number and ID?"

After slapping my ID on the desk, I told him the account number. I then tapped my nails impatiently on the desk as the guy typed my information into the computer and skimmed over his screen.

"Ms. Wright, I'm showing a transfer from one account to another that was done yesterday."

"A transfer?"

"Yes, Ma'am, There was a transfer of nine hundred and fifty thousand dollars from your Money Market account to your joint account."

My knees damn near gave out when I realized that I'd obviously linked my secret account to the joint account that Germaine had access to. *Damn, how could I be so stupid*?

"What? So, you're telling me that Money Market account is completely empty?"

"Yes, I'm afraid so."

I instantly felt sick. "Transfer it back," I demanded.

"I can't do that Ms. Wright," he informed.

"Why the hell not?"

"Because the funds were withdrawn this morning by a Germaine Evans. We have here in the notes that although you all don't share the same last name, he's your husband."

I gave him a look of disbelief. "Who in the hell authorized the funds to be withdrawn?" I beat my fists against the desk. "How could you let him take my fucking money? Why didn't anyone call me? How could you all let him transfer and withdraw almost a million dollars without proper authorization?"

"Well, the transfer was done online. As long as the password to get into the account was correct, that transaction didn't need authorization. The money was sent to a joint account, with no restrictions against it. It wasn't set up to where we needed both of you to withdraw funds."

"You assholes! That was my fucking money! That was the money for my new life!"

Sure I still had money tied up in the label with my

artists, I even had money in another bank, but it was the principle of the situation. It was *my* fucking hard earned money and Germaine had taken it. “So, you people just let him walk out of here with that amount of money? How did he get it, in cash?”

“Of course not. I wasn’t the one who actually did the transaction, but I’m sure he received a cashier’s check.”

“I still don’t understand how something like this can happen. I want a stop payment to be issued on that check now!”

The white guy seemed nervous. Like the information he was about to give would piss me off even more. “I can’t do that Ms. Wright.”

“Why not?”

“Because it’s the bank’s policy to only issue a stop payment if the actual check was lost or stolen.”

“Hell, it was stolen! He stole my money!” I screamed.

It seemed as though the entire bank stood still. All eyes were on me as one of the security guards walked over to see what the commotion was all about.

“Ma’am, is there a problem?”

I turned to the salt and pepper haired guard who had his hand resting safely on his gun.

“You’re damn right there’s a problem! You bastards let my husband take my fucking money!”

“Ma’am, can you please calm down and let’s see if we can get someone to help you,” the guard replied.

I pointed to the frail white guy. “This guy has already helped me! He told me that my fucking money is gone!”

The guard frowned. “Ma’am, I’m gonna have to ask you to leave if you don’t calm down.”

“I want my fucking money!” I stomped.

Suddenly, the burly security guard grabbed my elbow and escorted me out of the bank. “Where is your car, ma’am?”

By that time, I was in tears. But they weren’t tears of

sadness. They were tears of pure anger. "It's over there," I pointed.

He walked me to my car then helped me inside. "You have a good day, Ma'am and be careful," the guard said like he really gave a damn.

I cried for nearly ten minutes as I thought about Germaine taking my damn money. Then I decided to call him. After grabbing the phone from my purse, I instantly dialed Germaine's number. It went to voicemail after a couple of rings of course.

"You muthafucka! You better give me my damn money back! You didn't earn any of that shit!" was the first message I left. "You know this shit ain't right, you son-of-a-bitch! If I don't have my fucking money back by tomorrow, I'm going to the fucking police and tell them everything! I'll have Tyrell's bitch ass investigated and both of you weak, punk asses will go to jail!" was the second message. On my third call, the phone went straight to voicemail which meant that bastard had turned his shit off.

"That's okay, you son-of-a-bitch! Kingston is gonna get you!"

I backed out of the parking lot like a professional driver and headed straight to Memorial Hermann Hospital. When I arrived, I had a hard time trying to locate Kingston's room because I didn't have his last name, but I did tell the receptionist he'd been shot. She pecked at her computer keys and informed me that three gunshot victims had been admitted; a minor, a woman and a man. I was lucky. After giving me Kingston's room number, I rode the elevator up to his floor.

Anxious to see him, I hurried to his room with a quick stride. When I arrived, he was laying on his side facing the window.

"Hey, baby," I spoke softly.

Kingston slowly turned onto his side and frowned as soon as he saw me. I walked over to the bed. I could tell that he was a little groggy probably due to pain killers. He seemed a little weak, but was responsive. I pulled a chair on the side of the bed and sat down.

"Baby, I need to tell you something. Germaine and Tyrell are plotting to get rid of you."

He didn't respond. He seemed to be ignoring me. I hoped like hell the news would piss him off.

"Baby, did you hear me? They want to kill you. You have to get to them first. I'll even pay you to do it."

Still, no response.

"Baby, I know you really didn't want to rape me, but I understand why you did it."

He gave me an awkward look then turned onto his back. "You need to get your crazy ass out of here. It's your fault that I'm here in the first place."

Finally he spoke. "I'm sorry about what Jalisa did to you. I don't want you to be mad at me. Let me make it up to you."

He flinched when I eased my hand under the covers and rubbed his thigh. "What the fuck are you doing, Niquole?" he asked.

"You love it when I rub your thigh with my soft hands. You told me that."

"Niquole, get your fucking hands off of me!"

I ignored him and continued rubbing his thigh inching closer and closer to his shaft. "Let me show you how much you mean to me and how sorry I am," I said.

Kingston tried to swat my hand away. "Niquole, move!"

"Baby, you don't mean that. That's the medication making you talk like that. Just lay back and let me please you."

"Bitch, stop!"

He twisted and turned when I placed my lips on the tip of his dick. I was getting a little pissed because he wouldn't get hard. That had never happened before.

"What's wrong? It's never taken this long before." I continued to lick and suck on his softness, but nothing happened. "That's okay, baby. I know what will work."

I stood up and grabbed his hand. Kingston fought back with all the strength he could conjure up to stop me from putting his hand down my pants.

"It's okay. You can touch me down there."

Suddenly, Kingston yanked his hand away and gave me a disturbed look.

"Okay, you don't want that? I know what I can do."

When I tried to climb on top of him, he pushed me off. "Bitch, you're crazy!"

"I'm just trying to make you realize that you love me."

As I was about to attempt to climb on top of him again, a nurse entered the room.

"Yes, Mr. Braxton?" she addressed Kingston.

I stared at him and noticed that he was pressing the call button on the remote.

"I don't want any more visitors." He turned to me with anger in his eyes. "And this one needs to leave."

I assumed he was referring to me by the serious look on his face.

"Ma'am, I'm gonna have to ask you to leave," the nurse addressed me.

Furious, I grabbed my purse and walked toward the door. However before leaving, I turned back to Kingston and gave him a sorrowful look. When he frowned and rolled his eyes at me, it was at that moment that I realized he really didn't love me. I was reliving my past all over again; my mother's boyfriends, Mr. Hughes and A.J. Were my mother and Jalisa really right all along? Was I always trying to make a man love me once again? What was I doing wrong for them not to love me?

"Ma'am?" the nurse spoke.

"Bitch, I'm leaving."

I stared at her for a few seconds then hurried out the door. On my way to the elevator, I bumped a few nurses and visitors. I didn't care. I needed to get out of that hospital. I boarded the elevator and pressed the main floor button then cried profusely as the elevator made it's way down.

When the elevator stopped on the main floor, I raced through the front doors and to my car. I knew I probably should've gone to my hotel, but for some strange reason, I drove straight to my mother's house. I'm sure she was gonna have plenty to say, but as furious as I was she could bring her drama. I was ready.

"What do you want, Nikki?" she asked after opening the door.

"Aren't you going to let me in?" I questioned when I realized that she wasn't. At that moment, my mother glanced over her shoulder then back at me. I wondered what she was hiding. It was probably her man. "What are you…" I stopped and gave her a puzzled look when I heard my son.

"Johnathan!" I yelled right before forcing the door open. There was no way my mother's weak ass was gonna stop me from seeing my kids. "You weren't gonna tell me they were here?" I growled at her then lifted Nathan from the couch.

"Germaine told me everything that you've done," she said before grabbing the cordless phone and pressing three numbers. "You will not touch these boys!"

"They're my fucking sons!" I yelled at her.

"Yes, operator, I have an intruder," she spoke into the phone.

I couldn't believe this bitch had called 9-1-1 on me. After relaying her message, she hung up.

"How could you do this to me? I'm your daughter!"

"You haven't been my fucking daughter since your father left. All these years, you were pissed off at me because of him. It's time that you know the true story. I kicked your father out because I found out he had another kid; same age as you."

My heart sank. "Stop lying!"

"I kept that secret because I knew you wouldn't understand since the two of you were so close."

"Shut up!"

"You see your sister all the time, Nikki."

"What in the hell are you talking about?" I asked with an overly curious look on my face.

"Niquole," my mother paused like she was about to relay some heart wrenching news, "Jalisa is your sister. She doesn't know either."

I nearly dropped Nathan. Jalisa? My sister? How in the hell could she keep something like this from me? I nearly vomited as I thought back to our night with Mr. Hughes when we were in high school.

"Are you fucking serious? How could you keep something like that away from me? You should've told me! You don't know what the hell Jalisa and I have been through together!" When I walked over to her and pried Johnathan from her leg, he started crying.

"You wouldn't have understood, Nikki and neither would Jalisa. When your father told me that he knew for all those years that Jalisa was his daughter, I lost it. I couldn't forgive him for that and I damn sure wasn't gonna forget. He had to go."

I didn't know what to feel or say. All I could do was stand there and stare at her with a blank look on my face. I had to get out of there before I did something crazy. I started toward, the door, but she stepped in front of me.

"I can't let you take these boys."

"What in the hell do you mean by that?" I asked with a

serious look on my face. "My children are going with me and you're not gonna do a damn thing about it!" Johnathan started crying even more. When I walked around her nearly dragging him in the process, her ass stepped in front of me again. "You need to move out of my way! All these years, you've been fucking lying to me!"

"You wouldn't have understood."

"How in the hell do you know that? You didn't even try to make me understand!"

"You need help, Nikki."

"I don't need any fucking help! I probably wouldn't be the way that I am if I knew the fucking truth!"

"You need to talk to someone. I can't let you take these boys. I'm going to do everything in my power to help Germaine get full custody of them even if that means digging up your past indiscretions."

I was at a loss for words. With my track record, I didn't stand a chance.

"Why is everyone always taking up for Germaine? He's not innocent! He's not fucking innocent!"

"Give me Nathan, Nikki, and you better leave before the police arrive."

I gave her a flabbergasted look then stared at my bundle of joy that was in my arms. I couldn't hold back the tears as he cooed in my face. They were no longer tears of anger. They were tears of sadness. I held him tight, kissed his cheek then slowly handed him off to my mother. When I pulled Johnathan into my arms, he was a little resistant.

"What's wrong, baby?" I asked through sniffles.

"Don't wanna go wit' you."

A knife instantly drove through my heart after hearing those words. After that, I had to let them go. The only ones who were able to give me unconditional love were being taken away from me. Besides, I knew it wasn't right to drag them into my mess. I didn't bother to look back at them as I walked to the door.

"Nikki, you know this is for the best. These kids need stability," my mother said.

"Y'all turned my boys against me."

"No, you turned your boys against yourself."

"Before this shit is all said and done, you or Germaine's parents will have custody of my boys. I'm gonna make sure that Germaine doesn't stand a fucking chance. While he was telling you about my faults, he should've been telling you about his."

When she gave me a curious look, I decided to let the shit hit the fan on its own time because I was positive that it would all be unfolding soon.

Chapter Twenty-Seven

Twenty minutes after leaving my mother's house, I turned in the Westin's parking lot. After slowly walking to my room, I took a deep breath and fell back on the bed thinking about what my mother had told me about Jalisa as well as the disappearance of my money. How could she keep such a secret from me? The bitch who'd tried to kill my man was my sister. Damn! Even worse, we'd kissed in high school. I couldn't help but laugh. The whole situation was a bit hilarious and damn near unbelievable.

However, the Jalisa situation was the least of my worries at the moment. I was more so pissed off about my money if anything. I needed my *money.* The more pissed off I got, the more I realized that I had to find a way to get at least some of it back from Germaine. There was no way his ass was just gonna walk away with my shit without me putting up a fight. Then it hit me. I'd even let Meagan's ass get away with blackmailing me for the money and still hadn't done anything about it.

"That bitch!" I yelled after jumping off the bed.

It was finally time for her to feel my size seven up her ass or pressed across her throat. She'd definitely fucked with the wrong one. Rushing out of the room and down to the lobby, I power walked to my car and peeled out of the parking lot with thoughts of Meagan's whereabouts on my mind. The first place I wanted to look was her house, but as long as she'd worked for me, I'd never been there, so I didn't have an address. Thinking about her employee file, I made a quick right and headed to my label.

During the drive, I kept calling her, but of course she wouldn't answer. I'm sure she knew I wasn't calling to see how her day went. Again, she played me, but she wasn't getting away with it this time. Even though Kingston had told me she'd spent all the cash, I still needed to see for myself.

I arrived at my label a few minutes later. After unlocking the door, I ran straight to my office and turned on the light. Ignoring Kingston's blood on the floor, I hurried to my desk and turned on my desktop. I needed that bitch's address…and fast. Luckily, I'd stored all of my employees' information in a secured spot. As soon as I typed in my password and allowed the computer to boot up, I skimmed through the list of names until my eyes landed on hers.

"See you in a minute, bitch," I said jotting down her information and dashing back outside.

I drove like a maniac trying to get to Camden Park Apartments on Woodland Drive. I was determined that her ass was going to give me my fucking money back.

Once I arrived at the garden style apartment complex, I hurried up the stairs taking two at a time to the second floor. Soon, I was standing in front of her door. I stood there for a few seconds as I listened to the sounds of Joss Stone coming from inside. If she was having a party, I was about to crash it.

I knocked as hard as I could to make sure she heard me. As soon as she opened the door, you would've thought she'd seen a ghost from her facial expression. But a few seconds later, she gave me a smug and drunken smile. That's when I noticed the wine bottle in her hand. To make matters worse, Meagan's blond hair was all over her head, her eyes looked like a raccoon from running mascara and her lipstick was smeared.

"You have a lot of fucking nerves showing up here,"

she slurred before walking back inside.

I took that as an invitation to enter. I stared around her apartment and noticed a few empty pill bottles tossed on the floor. By the way she looked and the evidence all around me, I wondered how in the hell she was even able to stand.

I wasted no time. "Where the fuck is my money, Meagan?"

She looked at me and turned up the bottle. After taking a long swig, she laughed. "What money?"

"Bitch, don't insult me! The money you blackmailed from me! I want my shit now!"

Meagan laughed again as if the situation amused her. "Ask Kingston," she slurred before drinking from the bottle again.

At that point, I couldn't take anymore. I ran up to her drunk ass, knocked the bottle out of her hand then slapped the shit out of her pale white skin. Deciding that I wasn't done, I shook Meagan uncontrollably before pushing her onto the floor.

I stood over that bitch and gave her a questionable look. "What are you talking about? Ask him what?"

"He just left here with your money."

"Now, bitch, I know you're lying. That's fucking impossible. Kingston's at the hospital. He was shot earlier."

"I know. I watched the ambulance take him away from across the street." She smiled deviously. "But that doesn't mean he couldn't take your money."

"What do you mean by that?"

"He has your money. When I couldn't get more, he took what I had."

"What the hell are you talking about Meagan? Besides, Kingston told me you spent it all."

She smiled. "You don't know Kingston very well, do you? He fucked me just like he fucked you."

"How could he have my money when he's lying in a

hospital bed?"

"Let's just say, he checked himself out earlier," she replied. "Look around you, Niquole. Look at me. He's been here."

When I glanced around the apartment, it did look as though it had been ransacked. "There's one thing that has bothered me about the rape."

Meagan chuckled. "Which one? Yours or my friend's?"

"Bitch, you know which one I'm talking about. Where did it happen? Houston or Dallas?"

"Right here in good oleeee Houston," she slurred. "I'll let you in on another little secret, too," she continued. "Kingston doesn't live in Dallas. He lives right in the heart of Houston."

Before I could respond, the bitch passed out. Her ass went down like she'd just been knocked out by a professional boxer. I stared at her for a few seconds in disbelief before rummaging through her apartment to see if she was lying. She wasn't. My money was nowhere to be found.

Walking back into the living room, I stood over her body. For some reason, I didn't feel sorry for her ass, and wasn't inclined to get her some help. "Bitch, I hope you fucking die!" I said, right before walking out the front door. I'd let someone else find her corpse.

Chapter Twenty-Eight

Confused about the entire situation, I drove around the city for at least two hours before I found myself turning onto my street. Against Germaine's threats I decided to go back to my house anyway. Since my goal was to see if he was crazy enough to hide some of my stolen money or maybe even the check, I hoped and prayed that he wouldn't be there. Besides, what else did I have to lose at this point? He wasn't known to park in the garage, so once I coasted into my driveway and didn't see his truck, for once my prayers were answered.

I hurried out of the car and to the front door, fumbling through my keys. I had no idea why I was so damn nervous since the money was mine anyway, but my hands wouldn't stop shaking. After finding the right key, I only managed to get it halfway in, before realizing that it didn't work. He'd obviously changed the locks.

"Fuck!" I yelled.

Not knowing what to do, I began to pace back and forth until suddenly thinking about the garage. Running to the side of the house, I quickly punched in Nathan's birthday and smiled once I saw the door slowly begin to rise.

His dumb ass forgot to change the garage door code, I thought before running inside.

However, as soon as I reached the door leading into the house, and tried to turn the knob, it wouldn't bulge.

"Shit! We never lock that door," I said to myself.

I scoured the garage looking for something to help me break in. Soon, my eyes landed on the hand saw that Germaine used to cut wood for the fireplace. I grabbed the Black & Decker cordless machine and quickly started it up. Despite being unaware of what I was doing, I managed to cut the door knob off and gain entry within a few minutes.

Realizing that the house alarm didn't go off, I raced upstairs to his bedroom and looked in every drawer hoping I would stumble upon something. Next, I went into his closet and even checked his shoe boxes, but still couldn't find anything. Rushing back downstairs, I stopped when I saw the door leading to the basement open. Wondering if it was open when I first came inside the house, I was just about to go down there, when someone grabbed my shoulder.

As soon as I turned around, my eyes bulged when I found myself staring down the barrel of a gun. "Kingston?" I gasped. "What are you doing here?"

I could tell that he was still in pain from the way he clinched his face every few seconds.

He forced a sinister smile. "Your bitch ass husband sent his flunkie after me."

"What are you talking about?"

"At the hospital. I was taking a piss when I heard my room door open. I thought it was a nurse or doctor checking up on me. When I opened the bathroom door, I saw that thick ass nigga holding a syringe. You finally did something right, Niquole. You warned me about them."

I knew he was talking about Tyrell. "What did you do?"

"I rushed his ass. He dropped the syringe during the tussle, but I put his ass to sleep. He's probably waking up now in my hospital gown."

I glanced at his attire. I could tell that he was wearing Tyrell's clothes because they were way too big for him.

"I have a job to finish with your husband and since I'm

here, I may as well kill two birds with one stone."

"Kingston, please don't do this!" I begged.

"You leave me no other choice. You've become too much of a fucking liability. I have to make sure that your mistakes don't catch up to me. I'm not going back to jail, Niquole.

"Back to jail?" I questioned.

"Just a few assaults," he replied.

I gasped again. Who in the hell had I fallen in love with? "Kingston, Germaine isn't here," I tried to prolong my death.

"I'll just have to catch up with him another time, but believe me. I will get to him."

I had to think of something. "Let me help you find him. We can get rid of him and still be together. I have some money left, so it won't be hard for us to leave the country."

"Oh, *I* am leaving the country but not with you," he chuckled.

I slowly closed my eyes when I saw him cock the gun. Memories of my dad taking me to the park, movies, Chuck-E-Cheese and the beach clouded my mind. I wished I could go back to those days. I wished I could turn back the hands of time and be with my boys.

"Drop the fucking gun, nigga!"

I opened my eyes when I heard Germaine's voice.

"Guess that nigga woke up and called you, huh?" Kingston asked.

Germaine waved his own gun. "He didn't have to. I was waiting in the parking lot the entire time. I saw when you came out of the hospital and jumped in a cab. I followed you here."

"Germaine, what are you doing?" I asked. "Put the gun down!"

"Yeah, put the gun down because I'm not putting my shit down!" Kingston yelled.

Germaine smiled. "No, I'm gonna get rid of this problem."

"Germaine, this isn't you. Don't do this," I pleaded.

The vicious glare he gave me sent chills up and down my spine. "You're right. This isn't me," Germaine said.

I blew a sigh of relief.

"Punk ass," Kingston huffed.

"Niquole, I think you should do the honors," Germaine smiled wickedly.

I freaked out. "What?"

"Come here," he ordered.

I slowly walked over to him never unlocking my eyes from Kingston's.

"Do you love this man?" Germaine asked me when I reached him.

I stared at him. I was afraid to answer.

"Answer the fucking question. Do you love him?"

"Yes," I answered with tears in my eyes. "Please don't kill him." I could tell that Germaine's heart crumbled.

"Then I'm not gonna kill him. You are."

Kingston tensed and so did I. I jumped when I saw the side door open and almost flatlined when Jalisa entered.

"How'd you get out?" I addressed her.

"Didn't Germaine tell you that Tyrell would get me off?"

I gave her a curious yet frightened look as I watched her walk over to the kitchen utensil drawer, pull out a butcher knife then walk toward me. Were they about to double team us?

"All y'all muthafuckas crazy!" Kingston spoke loudly.

"Nigga, shut up!" Germaine barked.

At that moment, Germaine grabbed me then placed my body in front of his. Once Jalisa stood behind me, I could feel the tip of the butcher knife in my back.

"What are you doing, Jalisa?" I panicked.

"You're about to find out," she answered.

I wanted to pass out when Germaine grabbed my hand

and placed the gun inside it.

"Germaine, what are you doing?" I cried.

"It's either you or him," he spoke. "Either you die or he dies."

"I…I can't kill him!" I cried harder.

"Niquole, baby, just turn the gun around and shoot that nigga," Kingston addressed me.

Jalisa pressed the knife harder into my back to make sure that I didn't listen to Kingston.

"Nigga, I thought I told you to shut the fuck up!" Germaine barked after grabbing my hand again and forcing me to pull the trigger.

I watched as Kingston's body and his gun hit the floor at the same time. I was stunned and most of all speechless once I saw blood oozing from Kingston's chest.

"That's how much I loved you," Germaine addressed me before placing his gun beside me then walking out of the house.

I couldn't move, but Jalisa made me. I watched her snatch Kingston's gun from the floor and stand in front of me so that Kingston's lifeless body was out of my sight.

"You have been a thorn in my ass for far too long," she spoke after pointing the gun at me.

It was time for me to save my own life.

"Come on now, Jalisa. Can we just talk about this?"

"What's there to talk about? You sent me to jail!" she barked.

"Jalisa, I'm sorry for what I did to you, but this won't help it."

"Yes, it will. It'll help me anyway."

"No, it won't, Jalisa. Please don't do this," I begged.

"How do you know what will and won't help me? Huh?" she said still dangling the gun in my face.

I could tell that something else was bothering her. "Jalisa…"

"Shut up!" she screamed. "All these years, you've been a selfish, inconsiderate, greedy, conniving bitch."

I knew it was a long shot, but I decided to use the sister card. "Jalisa, don't do this. We're sisters! You're my sister!"

She laughed. "Bitch, I know."

"What? You know? How long have you known?"

"Since we were sixteen."

"Sixteen?" I gasped, thinking that she knew we were sisters when we had the threesome with Mr. Hughes. "You're kidding me, right?"

"No, No, I'm not. I heard our dad and my mom discussing it one day."

"Why didn't you tell me, Jalisa?"

"You don't get it, do you? I don't like you. Actually, I hate the ground you fucking walk on. I was planning to get rid of you when you had me drive you to your label that day, but this son-of-a-bitch fucked up that idea." She kicked Kingston.

"Don't kick him. He may still be alive," I pleaded.

"Naw, he's dead," she assured after kicking him again. "I can't believe how crazy you were for him."

"I love him."

"Bitch, you loved everybody that showed you a piece of attention. It's called obsessed, Nikki. You don't know what love is."

"What does it fucking matter to you?" I lashed out at her.

"It matters a lot. Everything I wanted, you always had to have," she continued. "You knew that I wanted Mr. Hughes, but you had to get in my way. You got in my way when you introduced me to Germaine. You told me that he seemed like a nice catch and that I should go for it, but I never got a chance because you fucked him first."

"You knew we were sisters when we seduced Mr. Hughes," I spoke. I was grossed out at the thought. "Germaine wasn't in to you. He told me."

"But you knew that I was into him so he still should've been off limits. And as far as Mr. Hughes goes, you threw yourself at him to get the attention off of me. You knew he wanted me!"

"Jalisa, we're sisters," I said again.

"Then you should know the lengths that *I* will go through to get what *I* want. The difference between you and I is that I'm patient and you're not. You don't deserve Germaine. I did and I still do. Unlike you bitch, I'll make sure he's happy."

"I don't fucking want him!" I blasted at her.

"That's good. Then this should be easy with you out of the way."

"So, let me get this straight. You've been waiting patiently to find that curve ball that would get you in the game."

"Yep," she answered bluntly. "If you hadn't gotten in my way all those years ago then it wouldn't be like this. I'd have him."

"He didn't want you then so what makes you so sure that he'll want you now?"

"I'm your sister, remember? I'm gonna make sure that I'm always around."

Before I could respond, Germaine reappeared.

"Jalisa, the cops are on the way."

"Germaine?" I addressed him.

"We're done," he spoke bluntly with a fierce look then walked out.

Jalisa smiled deviously. "You see, dear sister, the tables have turned. It's finally time for you to pay for all your wrong doings. By the way, your prints are on that gun and residue is on your hands so now *you're* going down for Kingston's murder. I wonder what you'll look like in a prison jumpsuit," she said with a wink.

All I could think about after her last statement was how karma was truly a bitch.

"I also wonder how it's gonna feel to finally fuck Germaine after all my fantasizing," Jalisa continued.

"You bitch! Germaine will never love you like he loved me!" I screamed then patted my chest to let her know that it was *always* all about me. "You remember that while you're *trying* to make him love you!"

"Look who's calling the kettle black."

"You'll never be me!"

"I don't wanna be you," she smiled wickedly after placing Kingston's gun back on the floor.

Suddenly, I snatched Germaine's gun up, pointed it at her and pressed the trigger over and over again. Nothing happened.

Jalisa smiled. "There was only one bullet in there."

I had no reply for her after realizing that it all was planned. All I could do was stare at Jalisa and wonder what I'd gotten myself into. I was in a twilight zone, but her next words quickly brought me back to reality.

"Oh! I forgot. There's no need for you to worry, dear sister."

"Worry about what, bitch?"

"I'm gonna take good care of your sons…well my son's now."

TO BE CONTINUED...

THE AVAILABLE WIFE *PART 2*

In Stores Now...

The Available Wife
A NOVEL BY
Carla
PENNINGTON
IN-STORES-
NOW
-PICK-UP-
YOUR-COPY
-TODAY!!
The Available Wife
Part 2
Carla
PENNINGTON

CHECK OUT THESE TITLES
BY: Kendall Banks
Rich GIRLS
KENDALL BANKS
CALL ME 555-4917
One Night Stand
KENDALL BANKS
Another... One Night Stand
THE SEQUEL
KENDALL BANKS
WELFARE GRIND
KENDALL BANKS
BEST SELLING AUTHOR OF
WELFARE GRIND
Still GRINDIN'
KENDALL BANKS
Welfare GRIND
Part 3
KENDALL BANKS